KILL OR BE KILLED?

"Adams!"

He turned. It was the kid.

"Not you again," he said.

"Come on, Adams, I ain't afraid. Are you?"

"Don't—" Clint shouted, but it was too late. The young man was going for his gun, leaving Clint no choice but to go for his.

The younger man was slow, almost agonizingly so.

"Stop!" Clint said, his gun already out, but the boy wasn't listening. He continued to draw his gun, and if given the chance, he would fire it.

"Damn it!" Clint swore, and shot . . .

DON'T MISS THESE
ALL-ACTION WESTERN SERIES
FROM THE BERKLEY PUBLISHING GROUP

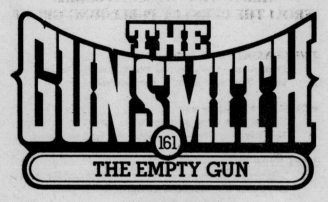

THE GUNSMITH
161
THE EMPTY GUN

J. R. ROBERTS

J
JOVE BOOKS, NEW YORK

THE EMPTY GUN

A Jove Book / published by arrangement with
the author

PRINTING HISTORY
Jove edition / May 1995

All rights reserved.
Copyright © 1995 by Robert J. Randisi.
This book may not be reproduced in whole
or in part, by mimeograph or any other means,
without permission. For information address:
The Berkley Publishing Group, 200 Madison Avenue,
New York, New York 10016.

ISBN: 0-515-11614-9

A JOVE BOOK®
Jove Books are published by The Berkley Publishing Group,
200 Madison Avenue, New York, New York 10016.
JOVE and the "J" design are trademarks
belonging to Jove Publications, Inc.

PRINTED IN THE UNITED STATES OF AMERICA

10 9 8 7 6 5 4 3 2 1

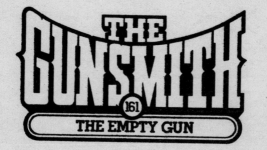

THE GUNSMITH

161

THE EMPTY GUN

ONE

When Clint Adams rode into Dawson City, Kansas, his intentions were simple. He had been on his way to Labyrinth, Texas, a place where he usually spent leisure time between his—for want of a better word—adventures. However, just outside of Dawson City one of his team horses came up lame. He had to release the animal from its harness, tie it to the back of the wagon, and then his big gelding, Duke, had to suffer the ignominy of being hitched to the wagon. Clint only did that because it was such a short distance to Dawson City. He never would have subjected Duke to pulling the wagon a long distance. That didn't seem to matter to the big gelding, though. Clint felt sure Duke was going to hold this against him for some time.

So as he drove his rig into town his intentions were to either give his team animal some time to rest, or trade for or buy a new one. He also wanted a meal, a bath, and a bed, not necessarily in that order.

As he drove down the main street he drew some attention, because Dawson City was actually no more than a small to middling size town. Also, the two horses pulling the wagon side by side were an odd sight to see. Duke's size dwarfed the other horse, who was obviously of far inferior quality.

He noticed a young man standing in front of the general store, wearing a gun low on his thigh. He didn't know why the man had caught his attention, but he had. And apparently Clint had caught the young man's attention, because he was shading his eyes with his hand, in order to get a better look at the stranger in town.

Clint wondered if he'd been recognized already. It was never a question of *if* someone would recognize him, but *when*.

As Clint stopped the wagon in front of the livery, a man came walking out, wiping his hands on a rag and chewing a majestic plug of tobacco. It was a toss-up as to what was the bigger swelling on his face, though, the plug in his cheek, or his nose. Clint had never seen a nose that big on a man before.

The liveryman spat a brown stream and looked the team over.

"Hell of a way to treat an animal like that," he said, looking Duke up and down a second and third time.

"Well, I didn't have much of a choice," Clint said, dropping down from the rig. "The other horse went lame."

"Wanna sell this'n?" the man asked.

"No," Clint said.

"Give ya a good price—even though he is gettin' on in years."

"He's not for sale," Clint said. "What I do want you to do is look at the other horse, and let me put up the horses and the rig at your livery."

"Have to drive the wagon round back," the man said. "Animals are welcome inside." He walked to the rear of the wagon where the lame horse was tied. "I'll untie this one. You take the wagon out back and I'll be along to help you unhitch those two and take 'em inside. You stayin' long?"

"As long as it takes for that horse to mend— that is, unless you got one for sale."

The man wiped the back of his neck with the dirty rag and spat another brown stream.

"Don't think I have."

"Can you think of anyone around town who might have a horse for sale?"

"Not offhand. You in a hurry to leave?"

"Well," Clint said, "I'm not going anywhere in a rush, and nobody's chasing me."

"Might as well wait for the animal to heal, then," the man said. "We got us a nice town."

"I'm sure you do."

"Hotel's nice. Tell 'em Warren sent ya."

"What does that get me?"

Warren frowned.

"Don't get ya nothin'."

"Then why should I tell them you sent me?"

Warren shrugged and said, " 'Cause I asked ya to, I guess."

Clint was getting too much of a headache from talking to Warren so he just said, "I'll do it."

Warren untied the lame horse. While he walked it inside, Clint walked the horses and rig around to the back, where he promptly released Duke from his embarrassment. The harness had been too small for his girth, and Clint rubbed the animal's sides with a brush he had in the wagon.

"I can do that inside," Warren said, coming out the back door.

"Just wanted to give him a couple of strokes. The harness was a little small."

"Don't think they make a harness to fit him."

"Probably not."

Warren unhitched the other horse and walked it inside.

Clint stood in front of Duke and stared at him, but the gelding looked away.

"How long are you going to be mad at me?"

Duke didn't look at him.

"Okay, come on, let's get you inside."

He walked Duke into the livery and found Warren looking the lame animal over.

"What do you see?" he asked.

Warren looked up from the horse's right foreleg and said, "No bone bruises, but he is walkin' kind of tender. I'll have to look him over real good."

"I'm going to collect my gear and go over to the hotel. I need a bath and some food. I'll be back after that."

"I should know something by then."

"I hope so."

Clint got his rifle and saddlebags from the rig and went back along the main street until he came to the Dawson City Hotel.

"Help ya?" a young clerk asked.

"Yes, I need a room." As an afterthought he added, "Warren sent me."

"So?"

"Never mind. Can I have a room?"

"Sure can. Nice one, too."

"Any one will do."

"Sign the register, please."

Clint turned the book around and signed his name, then accepted the key from the clerk.

"Room seven."

"Thanks. Do you have bath facilities?"

"We don't, but the barbershop across the street sure does." He smirked when he said it, which Clint didn't understand until later.

Clint rubbed his hand over his jaw.

"Guess I could use a shave, too. Thanks."

"Sure."

Clint went upstairs to room seven and dropped his saddlebags on the bed. His rifle he leaned against the wall next to the bed. He walked to the window and looked down at the street. Across the way he saw the young man he had noticed when he first rode into town. Had this man followed him? Was trouble already stalking him? He considered just staying in the hotel for a while, but he wanted that bath, and a meal.

He went back downstairs, through the lobby, and outside into the street, ready for anything.

Leonard Hollitt had recognized the man on the rig immediately—once he got a good look at him without the sun in his eyes. In order to do that he'd had to follow the man to the livery stable, wait while he made arrangements for his animals, and then take a good look at him when he came out. Then he was sure that Clint Adams, the Gunsmith, had just ridden into town—as if in answer to his prayers.

He finally knew how he was going to get done a thing he was too afraid to do for himself.

TWO

Hollitt had seen Clint Adams once before, up north in a small cow town. The boy had been waiting for a stage, and another passenger had pointed him out.

"That's the Gunsmith," the man had said. "One of the most feared gunmen in the history of the West."

Leonard Hollitt had been impressed.

"That man can't live a day of his life without looking over his shoulder," the other passenger went on. "Yahoos with guns are always trying to test him, and one of these days he'll run into somebody faster than he is."

Now, four years later, it was obvious that Clint Adams had not met that person yet.

Hollitt followed Clint Adams to his hotel and positioned himself across the street so that he'd see him when he left. His heart was pounding, but he knew he had to do this. There was no other way.

He folded his arms, watched the front door of the hotel, and waited.

When Clint came out the door of the hotel, he saw the man across the street. The man saw him at the same time and stepped into the street.

Clint cursed himself. He hadn't even had time to check in with the local law yet, and already there was going to be trouble.

Clint continued to cross the street himself until the young man called out, "Hey!"

Clint kept walking.

"Hey. Adams."

Clint stopped and turned to face the young man.

"Are you talking to me?"

"I am if your name is Clint Adams."

"It is."

"The one they call the Gunsmith?"

"So?"

"So go for your gun, mister."

"Why?"

"Why? Because that's what you do, ain't it?"

Clint stared at the young man. He was probably not yet twenty. He was scared, and sweating, so why was he doing this?

"Not today, son."

He turned to walk away.

"Don't turn your back on me."

Clint stopped, then turned to face the man.

"I don't want any trouble, son."

"Why? You yella?"

"I'm just not in the mood to kill anybody today—especially not some fool kid."

"I ain't a kid! I'm nineteen."

"What's your name?"

The man hesitated, then said, "It's Hollitt, Leonard Hollitt."

"Go home, Leonard Hollitt."

"I can't go home."

"Well, then go someplace else, but leave me alone."

"I can't do that, either."

Clint stared at the man, then walked toward him.

"Stop!"

It was Clint's experience that when you walked purposefully toward a man with a gun it made him hesitate. As you got closer and closer, he started to think about his own mortality. It was as if death was walking toward him. Most men preferred to do their killing from far off, so they couldn't see the man's face.

"Stop, or draw."

Clint kept walking, and the young man named Leonard Hollitt began to fidget. He looked around, as if seeking counsel from someone, and when he looked back Clint Adams was almost upon him.

"Hey—"

Clint hit the man once in the jaw with his fist. The blow stunned and surprised Hollitt, who staggered back a few feet and then went down. He was tall, but had a lot of filling out to do. His skinny neck did not help him absorb the blow, and he sat on his butt in the street, dazed.

"When you get some sense back, think about this," Clint said. "You could be lying in the street dead instead of just sitting there."

THREE

Before going for a bath, a shave, a drink, or a meal, Clint walked over to the sheriff's office.

"Can I help you?" The sheriff was a young man, probably late twenties. Clint was willing to bet he hadn't been a lawman a long time. As soon as Clint entered, the man had stood up from behind his desk and come around with his hand out. The number of lawmen Clint had seen do that he could count on the fingers of one hand.

"Sheriff, my name's Clint Adams."

"Glad to meet you," the man said. "My name's Andy Kale—Sheriff Andy Kale, that is. Just ride into town?"

"That's right."

"Well, what can I do for you, Mr. Adams?"

"Well . . ." Clint hated having to start off conversations telling somebody who he was. It didn't happen often, because he had the kind of name and reputation that stuck with people. The fact that this sheriff didn't recognize him just reinforced his belief that the man hadn't had the job for very long. "There's a young man in town who's been dogging me ever since I got here, Sheriff."

"Oh? Why's that?"

"He wants to draw against me."

"Oh. Well, that's bad. What's the young fella's name?"

"He told me his name is Leonard Hollitt."

"I don't know him. Is he a lawbreaker, do you think?"

"He's about nineteen, didn't strike me as that type. I think he's just full of piss and vinegar and wants to prove something by drawing against me."

"I guess I oughta talk to him."

"No, that's not why I came. I just wanted to let you know I was in your town and I'm not looking for trouble . . . and I wanted to let you know that this fella Hollitt and me had already had a little set-to in the street."

"Did he assault you?"

"I knocked him down, rather than draw on him."

"I can't blame you for that," Kale said. "I hate to use my gun, myself."

It was actually refreshing for Clint to be talking to someone who didn't recognize his name—he just wished it wasn't a lawman.

"Sheriff, I don't think you're understanding me. See, I have a reputation, and this young fellow apparently wants to try me out. I guess he recognized me when I rode in a little while ago."

A sheepish grin spread across the sheriff's face.

"I guess I should be embarrassed, then, for not recognizing you."

"I thought you might recognize my name."

The man spread his hands helplessly and said, "Sorry."

"Clint Adams."

"Still doesn't ring a bell."

Clint closed his eyes.

"Some people call me . . . the Gunsmith."

He hadn't called himself that very often over the years, and it felt sort of . . . silly.

"The Gunsmi—hey, wait a minute. I know who you are. You're . . . the Gunsmith."

"That's what I just said."

"Yeah, but . . . you've got a reputation!" Sheriff Andy Kale was wide-eyed now.

"I already told you that, too."

"Well . . . gee, Mr. Adams, I'm, uh, glad you came in to see me," Kale stammered.

"Sheriff, you mind if I ask you a question?"

"Uh, sure, go ahead—I mean, uh, no, go ahead and ask."

"How long have you had this job?"

"Uh . . . well, not long, really. I'm just sort of, uh, temporary. See, our sheriff died a few weeks back."

"Killed?"

"No, he had a heart attack. Doc was surprised, because Sheriff Mantle was only fifty."

"Uh-huh."

"The town council was looking for somebody to step in and take his place until the next election, and I volunteered."

"Do you have any deputies?"

"Well, no . . . that was a problem."

"Oh?"

"Yes, the deputies who were here working for Sheriff Mantle didn't want to work for me. I guess one or both of them thought they should have gotten the job."

"I see."

"So I'm alone . . . but it hasn't been so bad. There really hasn't been much trouble . . . until now, that is."

"What did you do before this?"

"Oh, this and that. I was a clerk at the general store for a while, and then at the hardware store. I worked as a bookkeeper for a while. I'm real good with numbers."

"Uh-huh." Bookkeeping. Real good experience for a lawman, Clint thought.

"Do you think you'll have much more trouble from this young fellow?"

"I hope not, Sheriff."

"Will you, uh, kill him if you have to?"

"Sheriff, I only kill when I have no other choice. I'm here because one of my horses went lame. All I want is a bath, a shave, a beer, and a meal. If I have to wait for the horse to heal, then I just want to be left alone."

"Well, I'll see what I can do, Mr. Adams."

"Just remember that I was here," Clint said, "that's all."

"Oh," Sheriff Andy Kale said, nodding his head emphatically, "I'll remember."

FOUR

Clint left the sheriff's office and paused outside to look the street over. He hated having to look over his shoulder for a youngster with a gun, but that was the price he paid for thinking himself a heller with a gun when he was young. Most of his reputation had been built in his twenties and early thirties until he realized that wasn't the way to live. Since then any time he was forced to add to his reputation it was done kicking and screaming.

He didn't see Leonard Hollitt anywhere so he walked back toward the hotel. As he approached, he saw the barbershop across the street from it.

He entered the barbershop and saw that there were two chairs, and they were both empty. The place was like no barbershop he'd ever seen before. For one thing it was the cleanest place he'd ever seen. There wasn't a lock of hair on the floor.

Also it was kind of . . . fancy. The chairs were red leather and ornate silver metal. It looked as if someone had spent some money putting this place together, which he found odd for a town like this.

There was a bell hanging on the wall and beneath was a printed sign that said: RING FOR SERVICE. Clint rang it and waited.

It took only a few seconds for a door at the back of the room to open, and he was surprised to see a woman step through. She was in her late thirties, a handsome figure of a woman with large, round breasts and hips, but a waist that was still trim. She had red hair piled high on her head, and a sprinkling of freckles across the bridge of her nose. Her mouth was wide, and when she smiled at him he saw that her teeth were very white. She was wearing a long dress that reached almost to the floor and covered her to the neck. It was green, a color that went very well with her hair and her eyes.

"Can I help you?"

"Uh, yes, I was looking for a barber."

"I am the barber. What can I do for you?"

He didn't answer right away.

"Is there a problem?"

"Huh? Uh, no, no problem. I just have never, uh, seen a lady barber before."

"Do you have a problem with a woman cutting your hair?"

"Uh, no, of course not. I'll, uh, be needing a shave, too."

"I think I can handle that. Would you like to sit in a chair?"

"Oh, sure."

He sat down, and she came over and covered him with a cloth that had blue flowers on it. Most barbers he'd ever been to tossed an old sheet over you—except for places like Denver, and San Francisco, and New York.

She moved around behind him with a comb and scissors, and he became aware of the scent of her perfume. It wasn't overpowering, which he guessed was why he hadn't smelled it from across the room. Up close, though, it tickled his senses. That coupled with the way she was running her fingers through his hair combined to give him a huge erection. He crossed his legs so she wouldn't see that he was making a tent with her cloth.

"Do you want it cut any particular way?"

"Uh, no, not too short, I guess. A trim, really."

"Fine."

He thought he'd talk to her, to take his mind off of her hands in his hair.

"I'll also be needing a bath. The clerk across the street said you had facilities."

"Yes, we do, in the back. I'll have someone draw it for you. Hot?"

"Yes."

"I'll take care of it."

She left him for a moment and walked to the back door again. She opened it, spoke to someone shortly, and then closed it and returned to him. She started touching his hair again, and his erection was becoming painful.

Suddenly she came around to the front and leaned against him while she cut his hair. He wondered if she did it consciously or unconsciously.

"I, uh, guess maybe I should have taken a bath first. Sorry if I'm a little . . . rank."

"Nonsense," she said. "You'll need the bath to get all of the hair off your neck. Besides, I like the way men smell."

Her skin was very pale, and he found himself trying to count her freckles.

"Let me know," she said.

"Know what?"

"How many you count."

Being caught embarrassed him.

"What's your name?" she asked.

"Clint Adams."

"May I call you Clint?"

"Sure."

"My name is Amanda."

"I'm pleased to meet you, Amanda."

"If you don't mind me saying so, Clint, you don't strike me as the kind of man who embarrasses easily."

"I don't . . . usually."

"Is this an uncomfortable situation for you?"

"To be truthful, yes."

"Why?"

"You're a beautiful woman, Amanda," he said, as she crossed in front of him to move to his other side. "Ah, being this close to someone as beautiful as you has an . . . effect on me."

"Oh," she said, and he watched her lips. "You mean . . . sexual."

"Well . . . yes."

"I guess I should confess, then."

"About what?"

"Well, I've cut a lot of men's hair. Young men, old men, boys, handsome men, some ugly men, some men who did stink badly. Through all of that, though, I've never gotten sexually aroused."

"I see."

"Until now."

FIVE

"What?"

He wasn't at all sure he'd heard right, or understood.

She moved around behind him and suddenly her mouth was by his ear.

"This is the first time I've ever wanted to fuck in this chair."

Clint caught his breath.

"Shocked?"

"Yes," he said truthfully.

"Well, so am I."

She moved her mouth away from his ear and started cutting his hair again.

"But I can't do it," she said matter-of-factly. Clint found himself feeling disappointed. He would have loved to have had sex with this woman in the barber chair. In fact, the thought of it excited him even more. He could almost see it in his mind's eye . . . and then he became aware that Amanda was still talking.

" . . . broad daylight and people would be able to see us through the window. They'd talk, and the women of this town would love any reason to run me out."

"Why is that?"

"Well, their men don't seem to mind having a woman cut their hair, but the women hate it."

"How have you managed to stay in business?"

"Well, we had a town discussion about it once, and I point-blank asked the women if they'd rather I open a whorehouse." She chuckled, a delightful sound. "They haven't bothered me much since then. Oh, they give me harsh looks in the street, but that doesn't bother me."

"You're a very strong-minded woman."

"Oh yes," she said, "I'm afraid I am."

"Why afraid?"

"Well, it gets me in trouble, sometimes."

She was cutting the back again and stopped abruptly. Suddenly, he felt her fingertips on the nape of his neck, just stroking.

"Amanda . . ."

"Oh," she said, taking her hand away, "I'm sorry. Would you like some bay—oh, no, you wouldn't. You're going to take a hot bath . . . aren't you?"

"Yes, I am."

She came around in front of him and removed the cloth, which was now covered with hair.

"Let me shave you, and then you can have that bath."

She shook out the cloth and placed it on him again. After that she pressed a hot towel to his face, then lathered him up and began to shave him with a straight razor. She was very gentle, but very sure-handed. He closed his eyes, settled back, inhaled the scent of her, and enjoyed the feel of her hands on him.

When she was finished, he was disappointed. It had been so relaxing that he wished it would go on.

"There," she said, removing the cloth again so he could get out of the chair. "Now you're ready for your bath."

"How much—"

"You can pay after your bath."

"Where do I go?"

"Right back there, through that door."

He could swear that there was a flush on her face that wasn't there before—but then hadn't she come right out and said she was sexually aroused?

"Joey will take care of you."

"Thanks."

He found himself wishing that Amanda was going to take care of him, but he went through the door and looked around for Joey. What he saw was a tall, pale-skinned woman in her twenties with long black hair, wearing a white robe.

"Hello," she said, "I'm Joey."

SIX

"Joey?"

"Josephine really," the woman said, "but you can call me Joey."

"Joey," he said again, stunned.

"Are you ready for your bath?"

"Uh, yes, I am."

"This way, please."

She led him down a long corridor lined with doors. As he passed one he heard the sounds of water splashing and someone moaning. He quickly realized that what Amanda had here was a very special business, apparently one that the women in town didn't know about.

She had herself a combination barbershop/bathhouse/bordello.

And Amanda was the head barber and madam.

"Right in here, Mr. Adams."

"Thanks."

He walked in and saw a cast-iron tub filled with steaming water. Next to the tub were a bar of soap, a brush, a sponge, and a towel. As he turned to close the door, he saw that Joey had stepped inside with him.

"Uh . . ."

"If you'll get undressed," she said, "I'll bathe you now."

"*You'll* bathe me? Now wait a minute—"

"It's all included in the price," she said, her dark eyebrows arched innocently. Her eyes were very dark, too, and her body smelled of a scent that was . . . clean. It might even have just been soap.

"Listen," he said, "when I came in I just wanted a haircut and a shave. I didn't know—"

"You've had the haircut and the shave," Joey said, "and now you're going to have the bath—and you're going to pay the same amount whether I bathe you or not. Tell the truth, would you rather bathe yourself?"

"Well . . . truthfully, no . . ."

"Then it's settled."

"I just don't—don't usually pay for—"

"Mr. Adams," she said, and her tone was scolding, "we certainly don't have to do anything you'd rather not do."

He suddenly felt very silly. He had had the haircut and shave, and he did need a bath. What was the harm in having someone scrub your back?

"Well, okay," he said, "I'll get undressed, but I'm warning you, I'm, uh, I mean I have a—"

"You don't have anything I haven't seen before, do you?"

"Well, I don't think so."

"Then get undressed and get in the tub."

She stood and watched him as he undressed, and he decided that if she was going to watch without embarrassment, then he was going to get undressed the same way.

He had been with enough women in his time to know that he was attractive to them, and he certainly wasn't ashamed of his body. He removed his boots first, and then socks, then took off his shirt. Last came him trousers and underwear, and as he removed them his erection came leaping into sight.

He looked at Joey, hoping to match stares, but her eyes were fixed somewhere else.

"Um," she said, "get in the tub, please."

He climbed into the tub, and she approached. She took hold of the soap and sponge and got on her knees next to him. He saw now why she wore the simple white robe. She was undoubtedly going to get wet, and since the customers apparently chose what they wanted, she probably wouldn't get naked unless he asked her to. Of course, since the material of her robe was very thin, once she got wet she probably might as well have been naked.

He sat in the hot water and closed his eyes. The heat felt good, but he was still very aware of his erection. He looked down and saw that the head of his penis poked out from the water—but if she didn't mind, he didn't either.

She soaped his back and shoulders, doing it slowly and deliberately, pushing her hand underwater so she could stroke his lower back and the upper slopes of his buttocks.

"Uh," he said, becoming embarrassed again in spite of his determination not to, "are you going to wash, uh, all over?"

"Unless you object."

Finally he turned and took the soap and sponge from her.

"It's not that I object, Joey, really. It's just that I didn't come here to pay for sex, and if I let you touch me anymore—I mean, I think I ought to wash, uh, certain parts of me myself."

She settled back onto her knees, looked at him steadily, and said, "That's up to you, Mr. Adams."

He started washing his butt and said, "Could you call me Clint?"

"If that's what you want. After all, you're paying."

Suddenly he realized that she was either hurt, or was faking feeling hurt.

"Please don't take this personally, Joey. You're a lovely woman."

"But you don't want me?"

"It's not that."

"For money, then."

"That's it," he said. "See, when I make love with a woman, I want it to be because she *wants* to make love with me."

"With?" she asked. She looked bewildered.

"What?"

"You said 'make love with'?"

"That's right. Why?"

"Most men don't even say 'make love' and when they do, they say 'make love to' not 'with.' "

"Well, sex is something that two people do together, not something that one person does to another. At least, that's the way I look at it."

"It's very unusual to find a man who looks at it that way, believe me."

"Well, I think that's sad."

He leaned back in the tub to wash between his legs and saw her looking down at him.

"You know, we were both wrong," she said.

"About what?"

"About you not having anything I haven't seen before."

"I don't—"

She reached into the tub slowly, so slowly that he found himself just watching her, and not trying to stop her.

"You're pretty," she said, touching the head of his penis, "here. Most men aren't pretty."

"Joey—" he said warningly.

She took her hand away and abruptly stood up. In a second she had dropped her gown to the floor. Her body was full and firm, big breasts and hips, a round belly, full thighs, and a thick patch of hair between her legs. Her nipples were large and thick, already distended.

"Joey—"

"Clint, would you please make love with me?" she asked.

"Joey—"

"I won't tell," she said. She lifted one leg into the tub, then the other, and then she was sitting opposite him. She splashed water all over herself so that her skin glistened.

"I'm asking you," she said, reaching out and

encircling him now with one hand. "Please . . . not for money . . . just for . . . us?"

Jesus, he thought, whether or not this could be called "paying for it," things had gone too far to stop now.

Way too far.

SEVEN

Leonard Hollitt had picked himself up off the street, brushed himself off, and then gone and gotten himself a few drinks. It had almost happened, but Adams had refused to draw his gun. Well, he'd just have to make him draw next time, not give him a choice at all.

After a few drinks he came out of the saloon and saw Clint Adams walking across the street. He watched Clint head into the barbershop. Hollitt decided to wait until he came out to try again.

After all, how long could it take to get a haircut?

He was still waiting an hour later.

While Joey was drying Clint off with a huge, white, fluffy towel, his penis started to swell again.

"Oh my," she said, "already?"

29

They had spent enough time in the tub together for the water to become tepid and Clint's skin to start to wrinkle. Joey, however, came out of the tub looking the way she had when she got in, her skin all smooth and white and glowing. Now she was on her knees in front of him, drying him, feeling him swell through the towel. Suddenly, she tossed the towel away and he was in her mouth.

"Jesus—" he said, putting his hands on her shoulders while she sucked him. Her mouth was avid and insistent, and she didn't stop until he exploded into her mouth, rising up on his toes and then groaning as he ejaculated. . . .

When Clint walked through the door back into the barbershop, Amanda was there waiting.

"You look . . . refreshed."

He was refreshed from the bath, but his legs were weak from Joey's bathing technique.

"How much do I owe you, Amanda?"

She told him.

"Seems worth it," he said, paying her.

"Come back anytime," she said, sliding into one of the barber chairs, rubbing her palms over the arms. "I'll keep a chair open for you."

Clint eyed Amanda and wondered, as wonderful as Joey had been in the tub, what it would have been like with the redhead.

Maybe another time he'd find out.

EIGHT

When Clint came out of the barbershop, he stood there for a moment taking a deep breath. He had certainly gotten more than he bargained for when he went in. Joey had been so good that he could hardly be sorry that he'd accepted her offer of making love together. He decided not to dwell on the fact that she was a prostitute and that he had done something he had only done once or twice before, and then in his youth. At his age he felt that paying for sex was a waste of money.

Of course, there were exceptions to every rule. The haircut, the shave, and the bath . . . well, no man could resist, and that was the truth of it. He had enjoyed it, and it was done.

He stepped down off the boardwalk to cross the street and heard someone call his name.

"Adams!"

He turned. It was the kid again.

"Not you again," he said.

"This time I ain't lettin' you get close to me, Adams," Leonard Hollitt said.

"Hollitt, don't make me—"

"Come on, Adams. I ain't afraid. Are you?"

"Yes," Clint said, "I am."

"What?" That clearly confused Hollitt.

"I'm afraid I'm going to have to kill you, boy."

"Well," Hollitt said, his voice betraying his nervousness, "maybe it will happen the other way around."

"Son," Clint said, "don't do it, I'm begging you."

"And I'm begging you," Hollitt said, "draw."

"Don't—" Clint shouted, but it was too late. The young man was going for his gun, leaving Clint no choice but to draw his.

The younger man was slow, almost agonizingly so.

"Stop!" Clint said, his gun already out, but the boy wasn't listening. He continued to draw his gun, and if given the chance, he would fire it.

"Damn it!" Clint swore, and shot Leonard Hollitt.

The bullet struck Hollitt in the chest like a fist. He looked down at himself, saw the blood running down his chest, over his belly. Where was the pain? he wondered—and then it hit him so hard that his knees buckled.

He opened his mouth and blood poured out. As he fell facedown in the dirt, he put his left hand in his pocket, desperately trying to pull something out.

He died with his hand still in the pocket.

As Clint walked toward the body, a crowd started to form, and then Sheriff Kale was there, pushing through.

"Mr. Adams," he said, looking down at the body of Leonard Hollitt, "was this the fellow you were telling me about?"

"Yes," Clint said, holstering his gun. "He braced me coming out of the barbershop and didn't give me any choice."

"That's the case, Sheriff," a man spoke up, "pure and simple. The boy didn't give him a choice."

"I saw it, too," another man said.

Kale leaned down and turned Leonard Hollitt over.

"He's dead, all right," the young sheriff said, feeling slightly queasy and not wanting to let on. "Looks like he's got his hand in his pocket."

Kale pulled the boy's hand out, then reached in and took out an envelope.

"It's a letter," the lawman said. "Addressed to the Hollitt Family, Winter Creek, Minnesota."

"A letter to his family?" Clint asked. "Why would he write a letter to his family and brace me without mailing it?"

"I don't know," Kale said. He handed Clint the letter, then bent over and picked up Hollitt's gun. "Mr. Adams?"

"Yes?"

"This is his gun, isn't it?"

"That's his gun," Clint said, with a nod.

"That's odd."

"What is?"

"Look for yourself," Kale said, handing over the gun. "It's not loaded."

"What?"

"It's empty."

Clint snatched the gun away and looked for himself. Sure enough, all of the chambers of the cyclinder were empty.

"What the hell—"

"Looks like this young man committed suicide," Kale said, "and used you to do it."

NINE

The crowd slowly dispersed as the body was picked up and carried to the undertaker's. Clint and Sheriff Kale went along with it.

"I don't understand it," Clint kept saying. "Why would he brace me with an empty gun?"

"Like I said," Kale repeated, "he committed suicide."

"But why this way?" Clint asked. "Why not just blow his own brains out?"

"I guess he didn't have the courage," Kale said, "although I suppose facing you amounts to the same thing. I wonder why he thought he had to do it with an empty gun. Did he think he might actually outdraw you by accident?"

"He was slow," Clint said, "woefully slow. There was no chance of that."

When they got to the undertaker's, Kale said, "I guess we'll have to bury him on Boot Hill with no marker—unless we contact his family. Maybe that's why he left us their address."

Clint was staring down at the letter in his hand.

"No," he said finally, "that's not why he left it."

"Then why?"

Clint looked at Kale.

"He wanted me to deliver it."

"What?"

"That's why he put his hand in his pocket before he died," Clint said. "He wanted us to find it, and he wanted me to deliver it."

"That doesn't make sense," Kale said. "He probably just forgot to mail it."

"I don't think so."

"Mr. Adams," Kale said, and then, "Clint, don't let guilt get the better of you. This boy didn't give you any warning. You did what you had to do."

"I didn't have to do it," Clint said. "I could have . . ."

"What?" Kale asked. "Talked him out of it? You tried that."

"But . . . his gun was empty."

"You didn't know that. You had no way of knowing that, no way at all."

"Still . . . there's this letter."

"Put a stamp on it and mail it if you want," Kale said. "What do you think his family will do if you deliver it and tell them that you're the man who killed their boy? Thank you?"

"I don't know. I only know that I have to deliver this letter."

Kale stared at Clint, then spoke in a softer voice.

"Get something to eat, Clint. Have a drink. Think it over."

Clint looked at Kale and said, "That's a good idea. I'll think it over . . . but I don't think I'll change my mind."

"Well, we'll bury him—"

"Bury him properly," Clint said. "I'll pay for it."

Kale gave Clint a helpless look.

"Just tell the undertaker to do it, Sheriff. Don't try lecturing me."

Kale threw up his hands and said, "All right, I'll talk to him."

"Let me know what the cost will be."

Kale nodded, and Clint turned and left with the letter clutched in his hand.

Suicide.

As he walked back to his hotel, he knew that the sheriff was right. Leonard Hollitt had picked Clint Adams to kill him, because he didn't have the courage to do it himself. What drove such a young man to suicide, Clint wondered, no matter how he did it?

He had to go to Minnesota, not only to deliver the letter, but to find out the answer to that question.

TEN

Clint spent the rest of the day berating himself over the incident. Maybe if he'd bothered to talk to Hollitt a little more . . . but no. The boy seemed to have his mind made up about what he was going to do. What would have happened, Clint wondered, if Hollitt had not recognized him when he came to town? Would he simply have chosen someone else? Maybe it would have been someone who wouldn't have concerned himself with whether the gun was loaded or empty, or with a letter in a dead man's pocket. What would have happened to the letter then?

Clint sat in the back of the saloon with a beer and the letter on the table in front of him. At one point he had almost convinced himself that he should open the letter and read it. At least then he'd know if it was important enough to travel all that way to deliver. In the end, though, he decided that the contents of the letter were none of his business.

He was still sitting there when the sheriff came in and sat down opposite him.

"How many beers have you had, Clint?"

"I lost count . . . after one."

One of the saloon girls came by and asked, "You want a beer, Sheriff?"

"Yes, Joan. And how many has my friend had since he's been here?"

"Him? That's his first."

That surprised Kale. He would have thought Clint had been sitting there drinking for most of the day.

"Take that one away and bring him a cold one," Kale said.

Joan nodded and took the half-filled mug of warm beer off the table.

"You should burn that letter, Clint, and forget about it."

"I can't."

"I know," Kale said, "but you should."

"I know."

Joan returned with two fresh beers and pouted when neither of the men paid any attention to her.

"When will you be leaving?" Kale asked him.

"Tomorrow, I guess," Clint said. "I'll be leaving my rig and team here at the livery."

"They'll be looked after." Kale shook his head and said, "I wish I was going with you."

"Why?"

"I've never been away from here."

Clint looked across the table at the younger man.

"They need you here."

"When you come back for your property," Kale asked, "will you tell me what happened?"

"I'll fill you in."

"Oh, by the way," the sheriff said, taking a piece of paper out of his pocket, "this is what you owe the undertaker."

Clint took the slip of paper and tucked it into his pocket without looking at it.

"Thanks, Sheriff. I'll be sure to take care of it before I leave."

Kale picked up his mug and drained half of it. He left the rest and stood up.

"I'm sorry this happened to you in our town, Clint. Maybe if I was a better sheriff—"

"This is none of your doing, Kale. One of us feeling guilty is enough, I think. Don't you?"

"You're probably right about that. Well, I've got rounds to make."

Clint waved one hand and went back to staring at the letter on the table.

A little while later Clint went back to the hotel and found a message there waiting for him.

"It's from Miss Amanda," the desk clerk said with a smile.

"What's it say?" Clint asked.

"I didn't read it," the clerk said, looking insulted.

"Are you sure?"

The man scowled and turned away.

Clint turned his back and read the message. It

asked him to come by the barbershop after clos-
ing, and that was all. Since he was leaving the
next day, he decided to go over and see what she
wanted. It was late, and since the "barbershop"
wasn't a regular whorehouse, he figured they'd
probably be closed by now.

He left the hotel and went across to the shop. It
was dark inside, but he knocked on the front door
until a light was lit. Amanda came walking to the
door, wearing a diaphanous gown that revealed
the smooth slopes of her breasts.

When she opened the door she said, "Clint, I'm
so glad you could come."

"Your message was . . . mysterious."

She allowed him to enter and closed the door.

"I didn't want to tell you any more than I had
to to get you to come over."

"And now that I'm here?"

"I heard what happened to you today."

"It didn't happen to me," he said bitterly. "It
happened to that kid."

"From what I heard, you didn't have much of
a choice."

"Who did you hear it from?"

"The sheriff," she said. "He comes here for a
haircut quite often."

"I see. What else did he tell you?"

"That you were leaving in the morning. You're
going to deliver a letter?"

"That's right, a letter the boy I killed had on
him when he died. It's to his family."

"Do you know what it says?"

"I haven't read it," he said. "I'm only going to
deliver it."

"I'm sorry," she said. "Can I offer you some brandy?"

His first instinct was to decline, but he didn't think she had yet gotten to the reason she asked him to come over.

"A brandy would be nice."

"Why don't you sit in one of the chairs and wait?" she said. "I'll go into the other room and get it."

She went through the back door, and he sat in the same chair he'd sat in earlier that day for his shave and haircut. He remembered the touch of her hands on his hair, and the nearness of her lips to his ear. He remembered what she had said she'd like to do in that chair, only it was daylight.

And now it wasn't.

ELEVEN

Amanda came back carrying two snifters of brandy and handed him one.

"Well," he said, "we're back where we started."

"Yes."

"You know, I was really shocked to find out that Joey was Josephine."

He heard that same chuckle that had delighted him earlier, and it worked its magic again.

"I thought you might be."

"And then to find out what . . . what she wanted to do. I mean, bathe me and all?"

"So you really didn't know when you came here?"

"I thought it was just a regular barbershop—until I saw you, that is."

"I'll take that as a compliment."

"You know," he said, looking in the mirror,

"you really do give a good haircut. Do you, uh . . ."

"Give baths as well? No, not usually. I really just run the place."

"Do you own it?"

"Well, yes, I own it and run it."

"And how do you keep the women in town from knowing what's going on?"

"It's up to the men," she said, with a shrug. "If they want to keep coming, then they have to keep it quiet."

They each sipped their brandy, and then he looked at her reflection in the mirror.

"You know, you really had me fooled this morning."

"Did I? About what?"

"Oh, that business about the chair . . . you know."

"I don't understand."

"Oh, I thought you were serious, and you were just, you know, getting me, uh, ready to go in the back . . . weren't you?"

"Now what makes you say that?"

"Well, you just finished telling me that you, uh, don't give baths."

"I don't sell my favors anymore, Clint," she said, moving closer to the chair, "but occasionally I give them away to someone I like—someone who excites me."

She moved around behind the chair again and put her mouth to his ear.

"The way you do."

Once again he was sitting in that chair with a raging erection.

She took the brandy from his hand and set it
down someplace, then slid her hands down over
his shoulders and chest.

"Amanda, what did you ask me to come here
for?"

"This," she said, sliding her hands inside his
shirt. "I heard you were leaving town and I
thought we might not be able to follow through
on our mutual attraction." She paused, then asked,
"There is a mutual attraction, isn't there?"

"Oh yes," he said, putting his hands on her
forearms, "there definitely is."

"Oh, good," she said, "I'd hate to be making a
fool of myself here."

"There's no danger of that," he assured her.

He took hold of her arms and pulled her around
to the front of the chair. She straddled his lap,
opened his shirt, and kissed his chest. She made
wet circles around his nipples with her tongue,
and then bit them lightly.

He lifted her face so he could kiss her, running
his tongue over her very white teeth. Her breasts
were pressed hard against his chest, and he could
feel the fullness and firmness of them.

She sat back then, finished unbuttoning his
shirt, and pulled it off of him. He helped her with
her gown, pulling it down from her shoulders until
it was bunched around her waist. Her breasts were
very full as he hefted them in his hands. He held
them by the undersides, letting them rest in his
palms while his thumbs rubbed her nipples lightly. She closed her eyes and moaned, then reached
to undo his belt and trousers.

"I don't think this is going to work," he said,

and finally she had to slide off his lap so they could get his pants and underwear off. While she was standing, she let the gown fall to the floor and stepped out of it. That done she got back into his lap.

Now he was able to slide his hands beneath her and cup her buttocks. His erection was between them, and she reached down to caress it, sliding her fingers down further to touch his testicles as well.

He moved his hands and was able to slide a finger up along her pussy from underneath. She grew wet very quickly, and the pungent scent of her overpowered her perfume.

"Oh, God," she said, and lifted her butt up so that his penis would slide along there. Finally she reached between them, held him fast, and slid right down onto him.

"Jesus . . ." he said. She was hotter than the bath he'd had earlier in the day. He buried his face between her breasts, licking her there, slowly rolling first one nipple and then the other between his lips.

She began to ride him up and down. They were making two sounds. First there was the juicy noise she made by riding him, and then the slapping sound of flesh on flesh as her butt came in contact with his thighs.

She began to move faster and faster, and he started coming up from the chair to meet her. She had her hands on his shoulders, and he was fascinated by the sight of her big breasts bobbing up and down just inches from his face. Every so often he would catch one in his mouth, or just make contact with his tongue on a nipple, and she'd moan. Apparently, she had very sensitive nipples, for just the smallest amount of contact with his tongue gave her shivers.

Finally he reached up to grasp her breasts and hold them so he could suck on them forcefully. She began bouncing up and down on him in a frenzy as waves and waves of pleasure overtook her . . . and he followed, exploding into her with such force that they almost fell out of the chair. . . .

"Jesus," he said, a little later as they got out of the chair, "I think I pulled a muscle."

They picked up their clothes and got dressed slowly.

"I never did that before," she said, while they were dressing.

He looked at her.

"I mean it," she said. "I've made love in lots of places, but never in a barber's chair."

"Well, it's a first for me, too."

When they were done dressing, she handed him his brandy snifter and they finished off their drinks.

"You'll be coming back this way, won't you?" she asked as she walked him to the door.

"I'll have to," he said. "I'm leaving my rig here."

"Well, make sure you stop by and see us before you leave again," she said. "Maybe the second time around we can get it right."

"I thought we got it pretty right this time, Amanda," he said.

He turned and took her into his arms and kissed her passionately.

"Be careful," she said breathlessly, when the kiss was over. "A simple thing like delivering a letter can get you killed."

He stared at her and wondered what kind of experiences she had gone through during her life to make her say a thing like that.

"I'm always careful, Amanda."

He went outside and closed the door behind him. As he was walking away from the shop he turned and saw that, if anyone had cared to watch, he and Amanda would have been spotlighted by the lamp inside.

It would have made for an interesting show.

TWELVE

The next morning Clint went to the livery to arrange to leave his team and rig there until he got back.

"That other horse of yours'll be healed by the time you get back."

"What's wrong with him?"

"Near as I can tell, I think he pulled a tendon."

Clint felt a twinge as he walked away from the livery and thought he knew how his horse felt. Making love in a barber chair might not have been the best idea he'd ever had.

Or was it her idea?

He told the liveryman to have Duke ready to travel in about an hour. From the livery he went to the undertaker's to settle up for the burial of Leonard Hollitt.

"He ain't kin of yours," the undertaker said, "why pay to bury him?"

"I killed him."

The undertaker looked at him funny and asked, "You pay to bury all the men you kill?"

"No," Clint said, "just the ones with empty guns."

After the undertaker's he went to the sheriff's office.

"Thought you'd be gone by this time, Clint," Kale said. Once again he came around his desk to shake hands.

"Just about ready to leave, Sheriff. Just wanted to thank you for coming by the saloon last night to talk to me. It was damn nice of you."

"Just trying to do my job right, Clint."

"I don't think so, but thanks, anyway."

Kale walked him outside.

"I wish you luck, Clint, but do you think you'll feel less guilt after this? Really?"

"I doubt it, Sheriff."

"Then why do it?"

He looked at the younger man and said, "I guess just because I feel I have to. If all I accomplish is to deliver the letter into his family's hands, and let them know what happened to him, then I'll have to be satisfied with that."

"Let them know what happened to him—does that mean you're going to tell them who killed him?"

"That's something else I feel I have to do."

"You're a braver man than me, Clint—braver

than most I know if you're going to admit that to his family."

"I can't tell them what happened to him and pretend I don't know who did it, Sheriff. I just wouldn't be able to do that."

"Well, like I said, I wish you luck. I think you're going to need it to come out of this with some feelings of satisfaction."

They shook hands again and Clint started walking back to the livery. On the way he stopped off at the general store and bought just a few things—some coffee, dried beef jerky, and a couple cans of fruit. He'd stop along the way whenever he had to, to pick up some more, but he figured if he traveled light he'd travel fast. A packhorse or mule would just slow him down.

When Clint got to the livery, Duke was saddled and waiting for him. The liveryman walked the big, black gelding out and handed the reins over.

"Are you sure you don't wanna sell him?" Warren asked.

Clint mounted up and looked down at the man.

"I'm sure."

THIRTEEN

To get to where he was going, Clint had to ride through a small patch of Nebraska into Iowa, and then north to Minnesota. Once there he started asking questions about how to get to the town on the letter, the town of Winter Creek. Armed with directions, he headed for what he assumed was young Leonard Hollitt's hometown.

Along the way Clint had forgiven himself several times over only to once again decide that he needed to do this as penance. Once he had delivered the letter to the family, he could ride away, because after that there was nothing else he could do.

Winter Creek was a small town, smaller than Dawson City had been. There was one hotel, called simply the Carlson Hotel—probably after the man who had opened it.

When Clint rode into Winter Creek, he didn't create much of a ripple. People went on about their business even as he rode down the main street.

He stopped first in front of the hotel and went inside. He wanted to make sure he was in the right place before he left Duke at the livery.

"Hello," the desk clerk said. "Can I get you a room?"

"You can if I'm in the right place."

"And where would that be, sir?" The clerk was in his forties, a small, slender man with brown hair and wire-framed glasses. "You're in Winter Creek. Where would you like to be?"

"Well, Winter Creek, I think. Do you know of a family in the area called Hollitt?"

"Sure. One of our finest families."

"Well, then, I guess I'm in the right place. I'll have a room."

"With pleasure. Sign the register, please."

Clint obliged him.

"Are you a friend of Anson Hollitt's?"

Clint hesitated, then said, "No."

"Maybe his daughter? Rachel?"

"No."

The man turned the book around and read Clint's name.

"I knew his son," Clint said.

"You knew Travis?"

"No," Clint said, "Leonard."

The clerk stopped short and paled a bit.

"Leonard?"

"That's right," Clint said, "Leonard Hollitt."

"I, uh, I don't think I know of a son named Leonard."

"Really."

"Maybe, uh, maybe you aren't in the right place after all, Mr. . . . Adams?"

Clint put his hands down on the desk and leaned toward the clerk, who backed away.

"You know something? Now more than ever I'm convinced I am. Can I have my key, please?"

Clint went up to his room, dropped his saddle-bags and rifle down, and sat on the bed. What was that all about? he wondered. Had the young man lied about his name?

Clint took the letter out and stared at it. It was addressed to Anson Hollitt, Winter Creek, Minnesota, but what guarantee did he now have that the dead man was indeed Leonard Hollitt?

Abruptly Clint slipped his thumb beneath the flap of the envelope and opened it. Before going out to talk to the Hollitt family, he wanted to see what was in that letter.

FOURTEEN

Dear Dad,
   I know you don't want me calling you that,
but I don't know what else to call you. If you
have received this letter it means I am dead. I
just thought you would want to know that.
                                   Your son,
                                   Leonard

Clint refolded the letter and placed it back in
the envelope. That was it? That was all Leonard
wanted his father to know? And what did he
mean that his father didn't want him calling
him that? Had he been disowned? Was that it?
So disowned that even the local hotel desk clerk
wouldn't acknowledge his existence?

There was a knock on Clint's door at that
moment. He took the time to put the envelope
back into his pocket before he answered.

"Clint Adams?"

"That's right."

The visitor was a tall, broad-shouldered man in his thirties who, by the looks of his face, had been in his share of fights. He was wearing a sheriff's badge on his shirt.

"Mind if I come in and talk to you?"

"Who are you?"

"Don't this tell you that?" the man asked, touching his badge.

"I mean your name."

"Sheriff Cactus Stone."

"Cactus?"

The man had the good grace to look embarrassed.

"My ma and pa didn't have much of an imagination. Can I come in?"

"Sure, Sheriff," Clint said, backing away from the door, "come ahead."

Stone entered and closed the door behind him. He removed his hat and held it. The gun on his hip was serviceable, nothing fancy, much like the man. His hands were big, with knobby knuckles and long fingers. Clint had the feeling that this man did most of his fighting with his fists, rather than with his gun.

"What did I do, Sheriff? I just rode into town."

"You ain't done nothin' that I know of . . . yet. I'm just doin' my job, talkin' to a stranger who just came to town."

"Are you here because I'm new in town, or because I was asking about the Hollitt family?"

The sheriff looked surprised.

"It doesn't take a genius to figure it out, Sheriff. The clerk said that the Hollitts were a fine family. I take that to mean they are prominent. Your presence here so soon confirms that. Are they prominent?"

"If prominent means rich, then yeah, they are."

"That's what it means."

"Look, Mr. Adams, I know your reputation. I'm just wonderin' why a man like you would be lookin' for the Hollitt family."

"I have a message for them."

"From who?"

"Their son."

"Travis?" the sheriff asked. "Why would Travis need you—"

"Not Travis," Clint said, cutting the man off. "I'm talking about Leonard."

"Leonard? You know, the clerk said you were askin' about a Leonard Hollitt."

"And you don't know him, right?"

"Never heard of him."

"Does that necessarily mean he doesn't exist?"

"Look," Stone said, "it's my job to know about the people who live here. Anson has two kids, Travis and Rachel. I don't know about no Leonard."

"Well," Clint said, "I do. I guess that puts us at something of an impasse."

"A what?"

"A standoff."

That he understood.

"What do we do now?" Clint asked.

"Well, now that you know there ain't no

Leonard, you don't have to bother the Hollitts."

"I told you, Sheriff," Clint said, "I know that there is a Leonard."

"And I told you—"

"I know what you told me. I intend to go out to see the Hollitt family and let *them* tell me that there is no son named Leonard."

"I can't let you do that."

"Why not?"

"It's my job."

"To keep me from talking to somebody?"

"To keep you from botherin' them."

"How do you propose to do that, Sheriff?" Clint asked him. "Are you going to arrest me for wanting to talk to someone?"

"No," Stone said, "I don't suppose I can arrest you for that."

"Then we're at another standoff, aren't we?"

The sheriff stared at him and then said, "An impasse, huh?"

"That's right, Sheriff."

"And there ain't nothin' I can say that will change your mind?"

"I'm sorry, Sheriff, no."

"Well, then," Stone said, replacing his hat, "I guess I'll just have to think of another way."

With that the man walked out, leaving Clint to wonder what that other way might be.

FIFTEEN

After the sheriff was gone, Clint took the letter out and read it again. What could Leonard Hollitt have done that he had been disowned so completely? He was only nineteen when he died.

Clint decided to try and find the Hollitts now instead of later, before the sheriff could even come up with a way to keep him from seeing them.

He went back downstairs, and as he walked through the lobby the clerk studiously looked away. Suddenly he heard Duke kicking up a fuss and rushed outside to see what was going on.

In the street two men were wrestling with Duke, obviously trying to get the big gelding to go with them. Duke, however, had no intention of going along and was giving the two men more than they could handle.

Clint took out his gun and fired into the air, because it was the only way to get the attention of the two men.

They both stopped and looked around, and froze when they saw Clint.

"Now take it easy, mister," one of them said.

"We're deputies," the other one said.

"Do deputies steal horses in this town?" Clint asked. "Let the reins go."

The men released Duke's reins, and the gelding immediately trotted over to where Clint was standing.

"Now drop your guns."

"Hey, wait—"

"Drop them on the ground—now!"

The two men exchanged a glance, then took their guns from their holsters and dropped them on the ground.

"Now kick them underneath the boardwalk."

"Mister, we told you—"

"Do it!"

Both men kicked their guns, one of them in total disgust. He was obviously upset that his weapon was going to end up under the walk, where it would be difficult to retrieve.

"That gun cost me a lot of money," he complained.

"Next time buy a cheaper one. Now, suppose you tell me what you were going to do with my horse?"

"We told you we was deputies—"

"I don't see any badges on your chests," Clint said, interrupting him. "Deputies don't wear badges in this town? Or is that just when they're stealing horses?"

"We told you we wasn't stealin' it."

"Then suppose you tell me what you were doing with it," Clint suggested.

The men exchanged another glance, but neither of them said anything. That was all right with Clint. He assumed that this was one of the ways the sheriff was going to keep him from bothering the Hollitts, by taking his horse.

"Go back and tell the sheriff it didn't work," Clint said.

"What makes you think the sheriff told us—"

"You said you were deputies, didn't you?"

"Yeah, but—"

"And I fired a shot and I don't see the sheriff rushing over here, do you? A good lawman would have been here before the echo faded."

"Yeah, but—"

"So go back to him and tell him it didn't work—and tell him he almost got you killed."

"But—"

"And don't forget to tell him to give you badges—if you really are deputies, that is."

The two men stood there staring at Clint, unsure about what to do next.

"Well go!"

"What about my gun?" The question was asked by the man who complained about how much his gun cost.

"You can get it another time."

"Mister—"

"You know," Clint said, "where I come from

we shoot men we catch stealing our horses, and ask questions later."

"Okay," the second man said, "we're goin'. Come on, Wade."

The first man, Wade, said to Clint, "You and me are gonna meet again, mister."

"You better hope we don't," Clint said.

The other man dragged Wade away, and Clint holstered his gun. It seemed that the sheriff was not going to be totally bound by the law in his attempts to keep the Hollitt family from being "bothered."

SIXTEEN

Clint's original intention had been to put Duke up in the livery, but after the incident with the two men he realized he couldn't do that. He decided that while he walked around town in search of someone who would give him the directions he needed, he'd have to keep Duke with him.

He did not find it very easy to obtain directions to the Hollitt place. Little by little he was able to put together a picture of the Hollitt family. Apparently their business was lumber. In fact, they were owners of one of the biggest lumber mills in the area, serving customers on both sides of the United States and Canadian border. Their presence in the area must have meant a lot to the town. That would explain the lack of cooperation on the part of the townspeople.

Late in the afternoon Clint decided to stop in the saloon for a beer and some time off.

He needed to come up with a different strategy. All he had gotten from the townspeople all morning were either blank looks or nasty looks.

He grabbed a beer from the silent bartender and took it to a table by the window. He did not normally make a target of himself this way, but he wanted to be able to sit and keep an eye on Duke, who was right out front.

It was unusual to find a bartender who didn't talk a stranger's ear off, so Clint figured the word had obviously been passed. There were only a few men in the saloon this early and they all ignored him as he walked to a table.

Clint nursed his beer and considered his options. He could saddle Duke and ride in each direction, searching for the Hollitt place, but how would he know when to stop riding? A mile? Five miles? Ten? That could take up a considerable portion of his life.

Another option was to drop the letter off at the post office and forget about it. Or he could drop the letter off and wait for someone to pick it up, then follow them.

His last option was to throw the letter out and leave town. Apparently Leonard Hollitt was not considered to be a son of Anson Hollitt—at least, not as far as the townspeople were concerned.

Did Anson Hollitt even know what was going on? If he did, would he approve?

"You two are useless," Sheriff Cactus Stone said. He was sitting behind his desk, looking at the two part-time deputies in disgust.

Wade Dixon scowled and looked away.

"You can't even steal a horse."

"That wasn't no normal horse, Cactus," the other man, Eric Wright, said. "He was . . . I dunno, he just wouldn't come with us."

"The least you could have done was untie him and let him loose."

"He wasn't tied to begin with."

"What?"

"He was just standing there," Wright said. "We tried to shoo him off, but he wouldn't move."

"We coulda got killed," Dixon said. "You didn't tell us who that fella was."

"If I had what would you have done?"

"I woulda killed him," Dixon said.

"With what?" Stone asked. "Your gun is under the boardwalk."

"I'm gonna get it back."

"Well, not yet you're not. What you're gonna do now is ride out to the Hollitt place and talk to Travis Hollitt. Tell him what's goin' on."

"Without my gun?"

"You have a rifle, don't you? Besides, what's going to happen to you on the way out there?"

"Look, Cactus—"

"Just do it, Wade. Tell Travis that there's a stranger named Clint Adams in town askin' about his father, and talkin' about somebody named Leonard Hollitt. You got all that?"

"Yeah, yeah, I got it."

"What do you want me to do, Cactus?" Wright asked.

"Just stay out of sight, Eric."

"Where?"

"Just hide someplace. Goddamn it, do I have to tell you everything? Get out of here, both of you—and don't do anything unless I tell you to. Just remember, Mr. Hollitt's not gonna like it if you mess up."

The two men got up and slunk out the door. Cactus Stone shook his head, more at himself than at them. It was a foolish idea to have had them try to steal Clint Adam's horse. They were right, Adams could have killed them. Stone knew that the people in town wouldn't give Adams directions to the Hollitt mill, but that didn't mean that Adams wouldn't find it eventually on his own. The only thing he could do now was wait for word from Travis Hollitt on what to do.

It never occurred to Stone to notify Anson Hollitt about what was happening. For the past few years Travis had been handling almost every aspect of the family's business. Travis and Cactus had been friends for years, and they both wanted Rachel Hollitt to marry Cactus. The lawman had been after her to marry him for years, ever since they were teenagers. He was five years older than Rachel, but he didn't think that was a factor. He couldn't for the life of him figure out why she hadn't yet consented to marry him, but he intended to keep on chasing her.

He'd catch her sooner or later.

SEVENTEEN

Clint finally decided that if he was going to stay in town he was going to have to take Duke over to the livery stable. Before he did that, though, he was going to talk to the sheriff and make sure that no more attempts would be made on the big gelding.

He left the saloon and walked Duke over to the sheriff's office. When he entered, he saw Cactus Stone sitting behind his desk. When Stone saw him, he stood up.

"Relax, Cactus," Clint said, "I just want to talk to you."

Stone remained standing behind his desk, eyeing Clint warily.

"Did those two morons you sent after my horse talk to you?"

Stone had the good grace not to lie.

"Yeah, they talked to me."

"You probably know that I haven't been able to get directions to the Hollitt place."

"I heard."

"I guess somebody spread the word, huh?"

"I guess."

"Well, somebody should spread the word again. If anything happens to my horse, anything at all, I'll be coming after you, Cactus."

Stone stared at Clint for a moment, obviously speechless.

"You're threatening a lawman," he finally said.

"I'm threatening you, Cactus, not that star on your chest. Because you're trying to keep me from seeing Anson Hollitt, it's you who are keeping me in town longer than I'd like to be here. I need to put my horse up at the livery. If anything happens to him while he's there—"

"Nothing is gonna happen to your horse, Adams," Stone said. "I wouldn't harm an animal like that."

"Glad to hear it."

"But I don't like being threatened."

"I don't like being here."

"Then leave."

"As soon as I've done what I came here to do, and not before. You can frustrate me all you want, but I will get to Anson Hollitt sooner or later."

"I guess we'll see," Stone said.

Clint turned to leave but stopped at the door.

"Those two said they were deputies. Is that true?"

Stone hesitated, then said, "They're part-time deputies."

"Well, keep them out of my way. I don't like them."

"Adams, I still think we'd all be better off if you left town."

"I know you do, Cactus. Unfortunately for you, I don't put much stock in what you think."

Clint left the sheriff's office, retrieved Duke's reins, and walked over to the livery with him.

EIGHTEEN

Travis Hollitt was in the office at the mill when he got word from one of his men, Bob Williams, that somebody from town wanted to talk to him.

"Who?" he asked.

"Says his name is, uh, Wade Dixon."

Travis looked at his foreman, Gary Lane.

"Do we know him?"

Lane shrugged.

"He says the sheriff sent him," Williams said.

"Cactus? Okay, Williams, send him in, let's see what he wants."

Williams left and Lane said, "We got a lot of work to do, Travis."

"This'll only take a minute, Gary. Cactus sent him, so it must be something important."

Travis Hollitt and his foreman, Gary Lane, were a study in contrasts. Hollitt was a tall man, six three, in his thirties, broad-shouldered, trim, clean shaven, and handsome. Lane, on the other hand, was built closer to the ground, five eight, thick through the waist and chest, very strong, bearded, and nothing if he wasn't ugly. He had been in love with Travis's sister for the past few years, but he knew he had no chance with her because of the way he looked.

Williams brought Wade Dixon in and left. Hollitt recognized Dixon from town, but would not have known his name if Williams hadn't told him what it was.

"You say Cactus sent you?"

"Yeah," Dixon said, obviously unhappy to be there.

Travis Hollitt gave the man's empty holster a brief curious look.

"What's it about?" Hollitt asked.

"Cactus wanted me to tell you that there's a stranger in town lookin' for your father."

"A stranger? Do we know his name?"

Dixon nodded.

"Clint Adams."

Hollitt looked at Gary Lane, who said, "The Gunsmith."

That name Hollitt knew.

"What would a man like that want with my father?" he asked.

Lane shrugged and said, "A job?"

"He don't want no job," Dixon said.

"Then what does he want?"

"He's askin' questions."

Hollitt looked at Lane, who asked, "Are we gonna have to drag it out of you? Questions about what?"

"Somebody named Leonard Hollitt."

Now it was Lane's turn to look at Travis, who simply shrugged.

"Cactus wants to know what he should do. Adams has been tryin' to get somebody to tell him how to get out here, but nobody's talkin'."

"That's good," Hollitt said. "Tell Cactus to keep Adams in the dark until I get there."

Dixon waited a few moments, then asked, "Is that it?"

"Yeah, that's it."

Dixon shrugged and left.

"What's going on?" Lane asked.

"What do you mean?"

"Who's this Leonard Hollitt? A cousin?"

"I never heard of him."

"Then why not let the man come out here and see what he wants?"

"I'm goin' to go to town and see what he wants, Gary," Hollitt said.

"I'll come with you."

"No," Hollitt said. "You said yourself we have a lot of work. You stay here and see to it. I'll be back in a little while."

"You're goin' now?" Lane asked, in surprise.

"Yeah, I'm going now."

"Travis—"

"I'll be back later, Gary. Just take care of things, all right?"

Lane had a puzzled look on his face as Hollitt went out the door. He was the foreman and he didn't like being kept in the dark about things. Old Man Hollitt had never done it to him, and up to this point neither had Travis.

He didn't like the feeling.

Outside the mill office, Wade Dixon mounted his horse and started back to town. Coming down the road from the other direction was Rachel Hollitt. Like the rest of the men in town, Dixon was a little in love with Rachel, and a lot in lust. Her chestnut hair was tied back in a ponytail, and it bobbed up and down as she rode toward him. At twenty-four she was a lovely woman, tall and full-bodied. Her skin usually had a quality to it that made it seem as if she was glowing.

"Hello, Miss Hollitt," Dixon called out.

She reined her horse in and stared at him.

"Wade Dixon," he said, realizing that she didn't know him. "I'm a friend of Sheriff Stone's."

"Oh, well, hello. Is Cactus here?"

"No, he sent me out to talk to your brother."

"Oh? About what?"

"Oh, somethin' about a man named Leonard Hollitt?"

"Leonard Hollitt? Is that a relative?"

"I don't know," Dixon said. "I thought you might. Seems there's some stranger in town looking to talk to your father, and Cactus don't want him to."

"Why not?"

"Damned if I know—'scuse me. I gotta get back to town."

Confused, Rachel rode her horse over to the office, where she saw her brother coming down the steps. She dismounted and ran over to him.

"I just heard something odd."

"What?"

"A man from town said there's a stranger who wants to talk to Dad about somebody named Leonard Hollitt. Do we know a Leonard Hollitt, Travis?"

"No, we don't, Rachel. It must be a mistake."

"Why don't we ask Dad about it?"

"No," her brother said. "I don't want anyone bothering him. I'm going to town now to find out what it's about."

"I'll come with you."

"No."

"Why not?"

"I want to talk to Cactus without him mooning all over you."

"Travis—"

"Just let me handle it, Rachel."

As she watched her brother walk over to his horse and mount up, she wondered what there was to handle.

NINETEEN

Clint took Duke over to the livery where the liveryman was sufficiently impressed with the big gelding that Clint knew that the man would take good care of him.

"You've probably heard something around town about me," Clint said to the man before he left.

"Somethin'," the man admitted. He was small, probably no more then five foot two, and his face had a hangdog look to it, like he was always sad.

"Whatever I do, and whatever happens to me, nothing better happen to that horse."

"Mister," the man said, drawing himself up to his full height, "I ain't never hurt a horse in my life, and I ain't never let a horse be hurt when it was in my care."

"What's your name?"

"Wilmer."

"I'm going to take you at your word, Wilmer."

"I give you my word, mister," Wilmer said, "I won't let nothin' happen to your horse. A horse that magnificent, it would be a damn sin."

So, satisfied that the man thought enough of Duke to care for him in the proper manner, Clint left the livery and went to the hotel to spend some time in his room, thinking things through.

Staring out his window at the street below, he thought about the barbershop in Dawson City. It was the only thing worth remembering about that town. He still hadn't found anything worth remembering about this one.

It was getting on toward evening and he decided that he wasn't going to find anything out tonight. He'd have to start looking again in the morning.

He left his room and was about to walk past the front desk when something occurred to him. He turned and walked over to the desk.

"Uh, yes, sir?" the clerk asked nervously.

"If anyone is looking for me I'll be at the saloon."

The clerk stared at him.

"If anyone asks, tell them. Okay?"

"Uh, sure, Mr. Adams."

"Thanks."

Clint left and went to the saloon. If people didn't want to talk to him or give him directions, maybe they'd want to try to take his money at poker.

When Travis Hollitt entered the hotel lobby, the clerk just about snapped to attention.

"Mr. Hollitt! What a pleasure to have you, sir—"

"Is Clint Adams in his room?"

"Uh, no, sir, he's not."

"Where is he?"

"He told me that if anyone wanted to see him, he'd be at the saloon."

Hollitt left without saying another word, but instead of going to the saloon he went to the sheriff's office, where he found his friend Cactus Stone sitting behind his desk.

"What's goin' on, Cactus?"

"What did Dixon tell you?"

Hollitt repeated what Wade Dixon had told him.

"That's about it, Travis. I didn't think you'd want him talkin' to your father."

"You're right, I don't want him botherin' Pa, but that idiot you sent out to me also told my sister."

"Doesn't Rachel know—"

"No, Rachel doesn't know anything, Cactus, and I want to keep it that way."

"Did, uh, did she come with you?"

"No, she didn't, so stop moonin' over her. Jesus, Cactus, when are you gonna get her to marry you?"

"I'm tryin', Travis!"

"Look, Adams is over at the saloon. I'm goin' over there to talk to him."

"Talk?"

"Yeah, just talk . . . this time."

TWENTY

Clint wasn't able to get into a poker game. There were two games going, and they each had an open chair, but in each case he was told that the game was closed to "outsiders," and that any empty chairs were reserved for any "regulars" who showed up. He decided not to push the issue, got himself a beer, and went to sit at a back table.

A lot of people looked at him, but no one spoke to him. Eventually, a man entered through the batwing doors, a tall, handsome fellow with a strong jaw. He stopped just inside, looking around, then walked over to the bartender.

"Is Clint Adams in here, Will?" Hollitt asked.

"Is that the fella the sheriff told us about?"

"Yeah, that's him."

"He's sittin' over in the corner, Travis."

"Where?"

The bartender jerked his head and said, "There."

"I see him. Give me a beer, will you?"

Clint didn't hear the words, but he got the gist of the conversation. The man then picked up his beer and walked over to his table with it.

"Mind if I sit?"

"Why?"

"My name's Hollitt."

"Have a seat."

Hollitt sat across from him.

"Are you Travis?" Clint said.

"That's right. I understand you been askin' around town after my father."

"That's right."

"Why?"

"I've got something for him."

"What?"

"It's for him."

"You can tell me."

"I don't think so."

Hollitt's firm jaw clenched.

"I handle all the business for the family now, Mr. Adams. Anything you wanted to tell my father you can tell me."

"My business is with him," Clint said. "In fact, it isn't business, it's something personal."

Hollitt sipped his beer and stared at Clint.

"Why are you bein' difficult, Adams?"

"I didn't have any reason to be difficult when I got here, Mr. Hollitt, but I've been shunned, glared at, lied to, my horse was almost stolen, and all because I wanted to talk to your father. Why is that?"

"The townspeople are protective of my father. He's been good to this town."

"I don't have any desire to harm him."

"You'll excuse me if I don't take your word for that, but you have a certain reputation. Suppose someone hired you to come here and kill my father."

"I don't hire my gun out."

"Like I said," Hollitt repeated, "you have a certain reputation."

"If you check, you'll see that my reputation is not for hiring out my gun."

"That don't matter. I'm here to tell you that you ain't gonna get in to see my father. Either you talk to me, or your business with the Hollitt family is over."

"I don't think so."

Hollitt sat forward and pushed his fine jaw out.

"I just said so."

"Sorry."

Hollitt frowned.

"What do you mean, sorry?"

"Can't do it."

"You mean you still intend to see my father?"

"Yes."

"You'll never get to him."

Clint smiled.

"I like a challenge, Mr. Hollitt, and although that isn't why I came here, I'm starting to get extremely challenged."

"You're making a mistake."

"Maybe."

"No," Hollitt said, nodding his head, "take my word for it, you are making a mistake."

"It's my mistake to make."

Hollitt stood up.

"And you'll regret makin' it."

"You didn't finish your beer."

Hollitt didn't answer. He just turned and walked out.

Well, Clint thought, at least he'd made contact with the family.

TWENTY-ONE

When Rachel Hollitt saw her brother heading out of the saloon, she ducked away from the window and into the alley next to the saloon. She didn't want him to know that she had followed him to town. Big Brother Travis thought he could order her around, but Rachel didn't take orders from anyone, and sometimes she went out of her way to prove that.

This was one of those times.

From the alley she watched her brother storm out of the saloon, and she could tell from the way he held his head, the set of his jaw and his shoulders, and the way he walked that he was angry.

She wanted to meet the man who was able to make her brother that mad.

She slipped out of the alley and went into the saloon. The man she had seen her brother talking to was still seated at his table.

"Miss Hollitt."

She turned at the sound of her name and saw the bartender staring at her. She didn't know his name, but obviously he knew who she was.

"What are you doin' here?" the man said. "This ain't no place for you."

"You obviously don't know anything about women . . ." she said. "Don't ever try to tell one where her place is."

"But Miss Hollitt—"

Rachel ignored the bartender and walked to the back table where Clint Adams was sitting.

Clint looked up and saw a beautiful woman in her early twenties with chestnut hair tied into a ponytail. She was tall, with wide shoulders that kept her full breasts from looking too big. She was wearing trousers and a man's shirt, and was filling both of them out nicely enough to attract the eyes of every man in the room.

"Can I help you?" he asked.

"That depends."

"On what?"

"What's your name?"

"Clint Adams."

She frowned.

"I know that name, don't I?"

"Do you?"

She was sure she did, but she couldn't place it at the moment.

"What's your business with my brother?"

"I don't know," Clint said. "I guess that depends, too."

"On what?"

"On who you are, and who your brother is."

"I'm Rachel Hollitt," she said. "My brother's name is Travis. You just sent him storming out of here very angry."

"Is that unusual?"

"As a matter of fact, it is," she said. "My brother is usually able to control his temper. What did you say to him?"

"Not much," he said. "That might have done it."

"I understand you've been asking around about my father, too?"

"I haven't been asking about your brother at all," Clint said, clarifying the situation, "but I have been asking about your father. I'd like to find him and talk to him."

"About what?"

Clint studied her for a moment, then said, "Why don't you sit down? You can finish your brother's beer."

"I'll sit," she said, doing so, "but I don't drink beer." She pushed the mug away from her.

"I'd like to talk to your father," Clint said, "and nobody seems to want me to do that—especially the sheriff, and your brother."

"Cactus?"

Clint nodded.

"I can't even get anyone to tell me how to get to your home."

"If my brother doesn't want to tell you that, he must have a reason."

"Not a good enough one, I'm afraid."

"Why do you want to see my father?"

"I want to ask him about someone."

"Leonard Hollitt?"

Clint was surprised.

"What do you know about Leonard?"

"Nothing," she said. "I never heard the name before today. Who is he?"

"That's what I came here to find out."

"Why?"

He took a deep breath and kept his eyes on her face when he answered.

"Because I killed him."

Her face didn't move a muscle. If she knew Leonard at all, if he was her brother, he felt sure some muscle in her face would have twitched, that she would have done something to betray her knowledge.

He was convinced that she didn't know who he was talking about.

TWENTY-TWO

"Maybe he's a cousin?" Clint suggested.

"Couldn't be," she said, with a shake of her head that made her ponytail jump around.

"Why not?"

"My father had no brothers or sisters, and neither did my mother."

The letter from Leonard Hollitt was burning a hole in Clint's pocket, but he didn't want to take it out and show it to her. In the letter Leonard called her father *his* father. If she didn't know anything about Leonard, Clint didn't want to be the one to tell her that maybe she had a brother she didn't know about.

If Leonard was a son that Anson Hollitt didn't want to admit to, that could only mean one thing—that the boy did not have the same mother as Travis and Rachel.

He was a bastard.

Clint sat back in his chair and stared at Rachel Hollitt. For all that he thought he owed to the dead young man, did he have the right to shake up this young woman's life? She seemed quite innocent and sweet.

In the end, though, if he could get in to talk to Anson Hollitt, it would be up to the old man.

"You know, only one person knows the real answer to this."

"To what?" she asked. "You still haven't told me what this is all about."

"That's just the point," he replied, "I don't know what it's all about. I want to find out from your father."

"But . . . what happened to send you here? You said you killed this Leonard Hollitt? How?"

Clint hesitated, then decided to tell her the whole story. She listened in rapt attention as he told her how the young man had stalked him and eventually forced him to kill him.

"Only now you don't feel justified?" she said when he was done. "You feel guilty?"

"Yes."

"Like there should have been something else you could have done?"

"Yes."

"It sounds to me like you did all you could."

"Would you say that if he had been a relative of yours?"

She hesitated, then said, "I honestly don't know."

"There's one more thing you don't know."

"What?"

"His gun was empty."

"What?"

"Completely empty."

"Then he had no chance, against anyone?"

"That's right."

"Well, that's all the more reason you shouldn't feel guilty."

"Maybe . . ."

"What makes you think my father can solve this for you?" she asked. "Didn't you ask my brother about it?"

"I didn't."

"Why not?"

"He came on a little too strong. He was too busy threatening me."

"Threatening you? Why would he do that?"

"I don't know," Clint said. "He seems dead set against letting me talk to your father."

"Well," Rachel said, "my father really hasn't been well lately—actually, the last couple of years."

"What's wrong with him?"

"He's getting old, I guess. He's just tired and listless all the time; he's lost interest in the business. Travis has had to run things alone since then—him and Gary, that is."

"Who's Gary?"

"Gary Lane, our foreman."

"What about you?"

"Me? Involved in the business? Travis would have a cow if he heard you say that. I'm a woman, or hadn't you noticed?"

Clint stared across the table at her, then looked around. She was still the object of a lot of attention in the room.

"Everybody's noticed that."

She blushed and looked away for a moment.

"Rachel, can you get me in to see your father?"

"After Travis said no?"

She struck Clint as a young woman who would have liked to be independent, and probably would have been if her brother wasn't around.

"How about just telling me where you live? I'll go out myself and try to see your father."

She studied him for a few moments, then slowly shook her head.

"Mr. Adams . . . Clint . . . I'd like to help you, really I would. I'm sorry that you're carrying around so much guilt inside, but I think I have to agree with my brother on this. My father is really not well enough to be upset."

"If Leonard Hollitt is not a relative," Clint asked, "why would he be upset?"

"I'll tell you what," she said. "I'll talk to my brother about it and see if I can't change his mind."

"Well, I guess I'll have to settle for that. Thank you."

"He might still be in town," she said, standing up. "Are you staying at the hotel?"

"Yes."

"I'll let you know what he says."

"Rachel, I hope this doesn't cause trouble between you and your brother."

"Oh," she said, "why should it?"

TWENTY-THREE

"You did what?" Travis Hollitt shouted at his sister.

"You don't have to shout, Travis," she said.

"What the hell did you think you were doing?" he shouted even louder. "I told you to stay out of it."

"Well, I wanted to see what it was I was staying out of."

They were in Sheriff Cactus Stone's office, and Stone was standing aside watching the argument between brother and sister.

"Jesus," Travis said, running his big hand over his face, "I can't believe this."

"Why are you so against Clint Adams talking to Pa, Travis? Do you know who Leonard Hollitt is?"

"No," he said. "I don't know who that is, but I don't want Pa bein' upset."

"Mr. Adams seems genuinely concerned with—"

"Shut up!" Travis yelled.

She took a step backward but said, "Don't tell me to shut up, Travis."

"Clint Adams is not interested in the welfare of this family, Rachel. That's my job."

"And mine."

"So what do you want to do?" Travis asked. "You want to let him ask Pa about some fella claims to have our name?"

"He's dead."

Travis paused a moment, then said, "What?"

"This Leonard Hollitt is dead. Clint killed him."

"Killed him?" Travis repeated.

"Clint?" Cactus Stone said. "When did you start calling him by his first name?"

"Quiet, Cactus," Travis said. "What do you mean, he killed him?"

Quickly Rachel explained to Travis what Clint had related to her, even the business about the empty gun.

"What kind of a fool goes up against Clint Adams with an empty gun?" Stone asked.

"A dead one," Travis said.

"Travis," Rachel said, "you did know Leonard Hollitt, didn't you?"

Travis stared at his sister for a few moments, then looked at Stone.

"Cactus, you mind leavin' us alone for a while?"

"This is my office, Travis—"

"Get out!"

Grudgingly, Cactus Stone left.

"Why do you treat him so badly?" Rachel asked. "He's your best friend."

"He needs to be more of a man," Travis said. "If he was, he'd be married to you by now."

"I don't want to marry Cactus, Travis, I've told you time and—"

"He'd make a good husband."

"Why, because he does what you tell him?"

"He could—"

"Wait a minute, wait a minute," she said, holding up her hand. "I don't want to talk about this now. I want to talk about Leonard Hollitt."

"Rachel—"

"You know something, Travis, I know you do, otherwise you would let Clint Adams talk to Pa."

"Rachel," Travis said, "you really don't need to know any of this."

"Any of what, Travis?" she asked. "Come on, I'm a member of this family, too. I have a right to know what's going on."

"Nothin's goin' on," Travis said. "Leonard Hollitt is just a fella who tried to get some money out of Pa a few years ago."

"Money for what?"

"He claimed that Pa was his father."

"What?"

"He came to town claiming that Pa knew his mother, and that he was Pa's bastard son."

"How old was he?"

"I don't know. About fifteen, I guess."

"Younger than us? Then he claimed that Pa cheated on Ma?"

"You see how unbelievable that is?" Travis

asked. "Pa would never cheat on Ma, Rachel, you know that."

"So what happened?"

"Pa gave him some money."

"Pa paid him? Even though he was lying?"

"I know," Travis said. "I didn't agree with him, but Pa said it was the only way to get the fella to go away."

"And did he?"

"Yes, and we never heard from him again . . . until now."

"Why would Clint Adams come back here after killing this Leonard Hollitt?" Rachel wondered aloud.

"Maybe he's after some money, too," Travis said. "You can see why I don't want him to talk to Pa, can't you? Especially the shape he's in now."

"Where was I during all this, Travis?" she asked. "How come I don't remember?"

"We kept it from you, Rachel, that's all. We didn't want to worry you. To bring it up now would just upset Pa. He'd start thinkin' about that, he'd start thinkin' about Ma . . . we don't need that right now. I need you to stand with me on this, Rachel. I need you to stand with the family."

"You know I will, Travis," she said, moving into his arms. "You know I will."

TWENTY-FOUR

Clint stayed at the saloon a little longer, wondering if maybe Rachel Hollitt would come back fairly soon. When she was gone an hour, he figured she wouldn't be back, so he left and headed for his hotel.

Travis Hollitt didn't seem to be the type of man who would change his mind, or have it changed by his little sister. Now that Clint knew what both of the Hollitt offspring looked like, though, maybe he'd be able to find their father by trailing them.

He decided that if he was going to follow someone it would have to be Rachel. There was too much chance of a dangerous confrontation with the brother.

He detoured from the hotel and went to the livery to saddle Duke. Hopefully, he'd be able to spot Rachel before she left town and follow her home. Hell, all he wanted to do was deliver the damned letter to Anson Hollitt and be on his way.

Why did everyone have to make it so goddamned hard?

After saddling Duke, Clint walked him over to the hotel and left him in the alley next to it, where he'd be out of sight. He found a wooden chair and set it against the front wall so he could sit there and watch the street. He couldn't see much of the town from here, but looking up and down the street he could at least see from the saloon to the sheriff's office.

As he sat down, he saw Sheriff Cactus Stone loitering outside his office. He didn't understand what the man was doing until the door to the office opened and Travis and Rachel Hollitt stepped out.

"What's goin' on?" Stone asked.

"Rachel is goin' back to the house, Cactus."

"Oh. Gee, Rachel, I thought maybe we could, you know, eat dinner together."

"I have to get back to Pa, Cactus," she said. "I've already been away longer than I said I would. Maybe next time I come to town, huh?"

"Sure," Stone said, "maybe next time."

"Go ahead, Rachel," Travis said. "I'll be home after I stop at the mill again."

Both men watched the young woman walk to her horse, mount up, and ride away, and then Hollitt struck Stone on the chest with the back of his hand to get his attention.

"Forget about my sister and listen up."

Stone turned his attention to Travis Hollitt, but he didn't ever forget about Rachel.

"I want you to watch Clint Adams close, do you hear, Cactus?"

"I hear you, Travis."

"If he somehow finds out where we live and starts that way, you head him off. Meanwhile, try to get him to leave town, because if he's still here at this time tomorrow I'm gonna take matters into my own hands."

"You can't break the law, Travis."

"Oh, Cactus," Hollitt said, "stop tryin' to act like a sheriff with me and just do as you're told. Understand?"

"Yeah, I understand," Stone said. "Travis?"

"What?"

"Will you talk to Rachel about me?"

Hollitt sighed. He was always talking to his sister about Stone, she just wasn't interested.

"Yeah, Cactus, I will."

"Thanks, Travis."

"I've got to see Mr. Hayes at the bank, and then I'll be leaving town, but I'll be back tomorrow. Clint Adams better be gone."

Clint saw Rachel Hollitt walk away from the two men, get on her horse, and ride toward him. He got up and ducked into the lobby as she rode by. Hollitt and Sheriff Stone stayed out front talking. If he tried to follow her now, they'd notice him. He waited until they'd stopped talking, when Travis mounted his horse and rode the other way and Stone went back inside.

He came out of the hotel then, mounted Duke, and rode in the same direction as Rachel.

TWENTY-FIVE

Clint picked up Rachel's trail just outside of town. She was heading north, and he hoped she was going right home. Since it was approaching dinnertime, he thought that was probably likely.

Eventually he came within sight of her and then simply started to follow her. He stayed far enough back that she couldn't see him with just a glance over her shoulder, but there was no danger of that since she never once looked behind her.

As it neared dusk, it started to get colder. He decided that if he had to stay in Minnesota any longer he was going to have to buy a jacket. He hoped that wouldn't be necessary, though.

They rode that way for about an hour before they finally came within sight of the house. It was a two-story structure with a corral and barn nearby, but there was no sign of any stock on the grounds. There were men walking around the grounds, however, so there was obviously work for them.

He topped a rise and was able to look down at the house, and at Rachel as she approached the front gate and rode through. As she reached the house, three different men rushed to take her horse from her. She dismounted and didn't seem to care which of the men took care of the horse.

Once she went into the house, Clint continued on. He wasn't sure what he was going to do, but he had to do something. The direct approach seemed to be the best bet.

He rode up to the front gate and found it locked. Apparently, this wasn't going to be as easy as he thought.

A man came walking up to the gate carrying a rifle.

"Can I help you?"

"Yes," Clint said, "I'd like to see Mr. Hollitt."

"What's it about?"

"It's a personal matter."

The man squinted up at him and studied him for a while before speaking again.

"What's your name?"

"Clint Adams."

"I'll tell Mr. Hollitt you're here. Just wait there."

Where else would I go? Clint thought.

He waited patiently while the man went to the house. He couldn't see much from where he was, though. He just hoped that the man would talk to Anson Hollitt, and not Rachel.

He hoped in vain.

The man came walking back toward the gate several moments later, accompanied by Rachel Hollitt. Her strides were purposeful, and she had a no-nonsense look on her face. Clint had the feeling that she was not on his side—not yet, anyway.

"Mr. Adams, what are you doing here?" she demanded.

"Miss Hollitt," Clint said. "It seems I stumbled upon the right place, doesn't it?"

"You followed me, didn't you?" She glared at him.

"Well, I have to confess, I did, yes."

"How dare you!"

"Now that I'm here, why not let me talk to your father and get this matter out of the way?"

"You want me to take care of him, Miss Hollitt?" the man asked.

He was in his early twenties, tall and slender, and he gazed at Rachel with the look of a man who is hopelessly charmed by someone.

"Paul," she said, "if Mr. Adams doesn't turn around and ride away in the next two minutes, shoot him."

The man looked shocked. Apparently that wasn't what he had in mind when he asked to take care of Clint.

"Shoot him?"

"Yes," Rachel said. "Shoot him right out of the saddle."

"Now, you don't mean that, Rachel," Clint said.

"Yes, I do."

"You do?" Paul asked.

She looked at him and said, "Yes, I do."

"Uh, Miss Hollitt, I can't do that. I mean, I can't just shoot a man—"

"He's on private property."

"Well, he is outside the gate, ma'am—"

"Paul, do you want to continue working here?"

"Well, yes, ma'am, but maybe we better ask your father—"

"You'll do as I say, Paul, or I'll fire you."

"That's not fair," Clint said.

"What?" she said, looking up at him.

Paul looked at him, too, with an expression of gratitude.

"You can't fire a man for not committing murder for you. Is that what your father would want?"

"Never mind what my father wants—"

"Miss Hollitt," Paul said, "maybe I should talk to your father—"

"No. My brother and I don't want my father bothered by this man." She looked at Clint and said, "If you don't leave, I'll shoot you myself."

"I doubt that."

She put her hands on her hips and glared at him.

"There are more men here. I'll find one who will shoot you."

"Okay, Rachel, okay," Clint said, realizing that they weren't getting anywhere this way. "I'll go, but I know where you and your father live now. I'm not going to go away."

"I'll tell my brother you were here," she said, "and he won't like it."

"You go ahead and tell him."

She turned to Paul and said, "And I'll tell my brother what you did, too."

She spun on her heel and stormed away. Paul looked up at Clint.

"I hope I didn't get you fired."

Paul shrugged and said, "Maybe I just should have shot you."

Clint smiled and shook his head.

"I don't think so."

"What's this about?" Paul asked. "I mean, if I'm going to lose my job over it."

"Miss Hollitt and her brother are just trying to keep me from talking to their father. Why, I don't know."

"Well, maybe you just better ride out now."

"Yeah," Clint said, "I guess I better."

Clint turned Duke around and rode away from the gate. He made one quick, wide circuit of the house to see if there was another way in, but there wasn't. He was going to have to figure something else out. At least he knew where Anson Hollitt lived now.

That was something.

TWENTY-SIX

By the time Clint got halfway back to town it was dark. He had thought about trying to find the Hollitt mill, but once the darkness fell he abandoned the idea. He'd have enough trouble getting back to town in the dark without having Duke break his leg.

When he returned to town he was going to have to try to come up with a plan to deliver the letter to Anson Hollitt. When he thought of the situation in those terms, as simply delivering a letter, it seemed absurd. But what if Leonard Hollitt really was Anson's son? Wouldn't a father want to know that his own son was dead—even if he were a bastard son?

Was that Travis's problem? But why should he feel threatened if Leonard was illegitimate? As the oldest son, Travis would surely inherit the business, wouldn't he? Was it a question of the family reputation?

As Clint finally reentered town, his head was swirling with possibilities, and his stomach was groaning with hunger. He decided to continue his thinking over dinner.

After Rachel Hollitt left town, Travis went over to the bank to discuss some business with the bank manager. When that was done, he mounted up and rode back to the mill. Even if Clint had been coming back from the house at the same time, their paths would not have crossed. It was a different route from the town to the mill than it was to the house.

During his ride to the mill Travis Hollitt thought back to the time when Leonard had first appeared. He'd just been a kid then, but an angry kid who could have ruined a few lives. It was worth it then to pay him off to get rid of him.

Clint Adams was a different story, though. This was a grown man with a reputation. Hollitt didn't think paying him off would do it.

Maybe killing him was the only answer.

After Travis Hollitt left town, Cactus Stone went looking for Clint Adams.

"Ain't seen him for a while, Sheriff," the desk clerk said.

"He's not in his room?"

"Nope."

"Damn."

Stone searched the whole town, but there wasn't any sign of Clint Adams. He went to the livery and found that the man's horse was gone as well. Could he have left town? Maybe, but probably not for good. It was more likely he was out trying to find the Hollitt house. If he simply traveled in each direction, eventually he'd find it, but maybe not tonight.

Stone decided to put a chair out in front of his office and wait for Clint to come riding into town again. This time he was going to have to be a little more forceful.

As Clint rode into town, he saw Sheriff Stone sitting in front of his office, but he ignored him as he rode by. He rode directly to the livery to put Duke up for the night and then walked back to his hotel.

"Sheriff was lookin' for you," the clerk told him.

"Uh-huh." Clint continued on up the stairs.

"Just a little while ago," the man called out.

"I heard you the first time."

"Ain't ya gonna see what he wants?"

Clint was more than halfway up the stairs by now so he ignored the man.

He went to his room and walked directly to the window. Sure enough, the sheriff was crossing the street, heading for the hotel. Clint didn't have much respect for the sheriff at this point. It was obvious that the man was friends with the Hollitt family—or more specifically with Travis Hollitt. They were either friends, or Hollitt was running the man. Either way Clint doubted that Stone was a very good lawman.

He decided to meet the sheriff head-on, see

how the man reacted if he were a little more forceful.

He was coming down the steps as the lawman entered the lobby, and Stone stopped short. He hadn't expected Clint to be coming back down again so soon.

"Are you looking for me again?" Clint asked.

"That's right. I—"

Clint kept walking right past the sheriff so that the man had to turn and trot after him.

"If you want to talk to me you'll have to come along. I need something to eat."

"Uh, okay, but I'm not eating with you."

"Good," Clint said, "because I didn't ask you to."

TWENTY-SEVEN

Clint took advantage of having the sheriff along by asking the man to show him where he could get a good steak. Stone took him to a small café off the main street that he probably never would have found on his own.

Once they were seated at a table, the sheriff agreed to have a cup of coffee.

"What's the relationship between you and the Hollitt family, Sheriff?" Clint started off with a question to throw the man off balance.

"What do ya mean? Me and Travis, we're friends."

"What about you and Anson?"

"I don't hardly talk to Mr. Hollitt at all."

"And Rachel?"

The sheriff looked down.

"It's no secret I want to marry Rachel."

"How does she feel about it?"

"We ain't married yet, are we?" Stone said sourly.

"Does it look promising?"

"I keep askin'," Stone said. "Eventually she'll say yes."

"You're sure of that?"

"Who else is there?"

"I don't know."

When the coffee came, Clint poured them each a cup.

"I'm supposed to be askin' you the questions," Stone complained.

"So go ahead and ask."

"Why do you want to cause trouble for the Hollitt family?"

"I don't."

"Then you'll leave town tomorrow?" Stone's look was hopeful.

"No."

"Damn you. Are you gonna make me get nasty?"

Clint had to smile at the man.

"Have you got a nasty bone in your body, Cactus?"

"Maybe not," Stone answered, "but if you're gonna do anything to hurt Rachel, I'll have to find one."

"Believe me, Cactus, I don't want to hurt anyone. I just want to talk to the old man."

"Travis won't let you do that. He don't let nobody do that."

"Not even for business purposes?"

"Travis handles all the business."

"When's the last time you saw Anson?"

Stone thought a moment and then said, "Must be over a year—maybe a year and a half."

"Maybe two?"

"Maybe."

"And how long since anyone's seen him?"

"About the same. Nobody I know in town has seen him."

"What about people coming in from out of town on business?"

"They deal with Travis, or with Gary."

"The foreman at the mill?"

Stone frowned.

"Rachel already told me about him. His name's Gary Lane?"

"That's right. Rachel told you that?"

"Yes."

They paused when the waiter came with Clint's dinner, a full plate of steak and potatoes.

"Where were you today?" Stone asked.

"When?"

"This afternoon, up to this evening when you rode back in?"

"I was out riding."

"I figured that much out," Stone said. "I ain't stupid, you know."

"I never said you were, Cactus. Who says you're stupid?"

"Well, Travis, sometimes—hey, I'm askin' the questions."

"Sorry, go ahead."

"Where were you—and don't tell me out riding."

"Okay," Clint said, "I'll tell you the truth."

"Good."

"I was out looking for either the Hollitt house or the mill."

"Did you find them?"

"I'll find the mill tomorrow."

"How are you gonna do that?"

"It's a business, Cactus," Clint said. "You can't hide a business from people. If you did, you'd go out of business."

"I guess that's right."

"So I'll just ride around tomorrow until I find a sign that says 'This way to the mill.' "

"That ain't what the sign says."

"Well, it'll say something like that."

"All that'll do is lead you to Travis again, and he don't want to talk to you."

"He's going to have to talk to me, Cactus, because I'm not leaving town without talking to Anson Hollitt."

"You're lookin' for a lot of trouble."

"What kind? Violence?"

"Maybe."

"Which side are you going to be on when that happens, Cactus? On the side of your friends, or the side of the law?"

Cactus frowned.

"Think about it, my friend—and let me get you a steak while you do it."

TWENTY-EIGHT

After dinner Clint and Stone went over to the saloon. Clint figured it was a surprise to everyone to see him walk in with the sheriff. It was a surprise to him, too, and, he was sure, to the sheriff.

As it turned out, Sheriff Cactus Stone was quite a simple man, with simple needs. He enjoyed being sheriff, and he wanted to marry Rachel Hollitt. From their conversation over dinner Clint decided that Stone felt that Travis Hollitt was the key to both of these things.

They each got a beer and walked to a table to sit together. The saloon was full, but people made way as the sheriff led him to the table. Once they were seated, Stone had his back to most of the people while Clint could see everyone and everything.

"You always sit with your back to the door?" Clint asked.

Stone frowned.

"Sometimes. Why?"

"How do you expect to head off trouble if you can't see everything?"

"Head off trouble? I usually take care of it if it comes up."

Clint shook his head.

"Your job would be easier and less dangerous if you got to trouble before it started and kept it from happening."

Stone thought a moment, then said, "I guess that makes sense, but how do you know if trouble is coming?"

"Well," Clint said, "the first step is to watch people. Change chairs."

Stone moved to another chair so that instead of sitting opposite Clint he was sitting to his left. From there he could see a lot more of what was going on.

"You've got two poker games going," Clint explained. "A poker game is always something to watch, because sometimes losers cause trouble, and there are more losers in a game than there are winners."

Stone nodded, listening.

"Also, watch the bar. The heaviest drinking is usually done by somebody standing at the bar. Especially watch for somebody who is drinking and can't stand still."

"Can't stand still?"

"Look at the fellow at the end of the bar. He can't keep his feet still, his head keeps swiveling around, and he's drinking with both hands. He's trouble waiting to happen. Watch him."

Stone nodded and watched.

"It's confusing a lot of people to see you and me here together," Clint pointed out.

"How come?"

"Didn't you pass the word that nobody was to talk to me about the Hollitts?"

"Well, yeah . . ." Stone said hesitantly.

"So now they see us sitting here together. I wonder what they're thinking."

"I don't know," Stone said, "and I don't care. I'm the sheriff, I can drink with whoever I want."

Clint wondered if, after tonight, some of the people in the saloon would be interested in talking to him.

"When were you a sheriff?" Stone asked.

"Many years ago."

"Not lately?"

"Not for a long time."

"Why not?"

"I don't have the patience for it anymore."

"What do ya need patience for?"

"Because sometimes if you wait trouble out it will pass on its own," Clint said. "But what you really need patience for is dealing with all the people you have to come in contact with."

"You mean strangers in town?"

"No," Clint said, shaking his head, "I mean the people who live in town, especially the people on the town council."

"Oh, the town council," Stone said. "Mr. Hollitt keeps them in line."

"Anson does?"

"Well, he used to," Stone said, with a frown. "Now it's Travis who does it."

"Travis has a lot of power hereabouts, I bet."

"Well, yeah, he does. Winter Creek depends a lot on the mill for its life."

"And so he gets his way."

"That's the way Anson was for years, until he started staying in the house."

"And now nobody ever sees him, huh?"

"Nobody but Travis and Rachel."

They drank their beers in silence, Stone dividing his attention between the two poker games and the fidgety gent at the bar.

"Cactus?"

"Huh?"

"Did you ever think that Anson Hollitt might be dead?" Clint asked.

"No," Stone said before the question really sank in. Then he looked at Clint and asked, "What?"

"Well, nobody's seen him in two years, right?"

"Uh, right . . ."

"And the only people who claim to have seen him are his son and daughter, right?"

"That's right."

"So, he could be dead for all anybody else knows."

Stone frowned and asked, "But why would they lie about it if he was?"

"To keep the mill running. See, people have been dealing for years with Anson Hollitt. If they heard he was dead, they might want to move their business to a different mill."

Stone thought that over for a few moments, then shook his head.

"I don't think so. I think you're wrong. Travis and Rachel wouldn't lie to me."

"They wouldn't?"

"No."

"Why not?"

"Because we're friends."

"Cactus," Clint said, leaning forward, "friends lie to friends all the time."

Stone was pondering that when a man Clint recognized walked in the door.

"I see somebody I want to talk to, Cactus. Thanks for not treating me like the town leper."

Clint got up to leave the table. Stone appeared so involved with his question about Anson being alive or dead that he seemed to have forgotten that he wanted Clint to leave town tomorrow.

Clint walked up to the bar to talk to the man who had just entered the saloon, the man he'd met that afternoon at the Hollitt house.

He hoped Paul hadn't gotten fired after all.

TWENTY-NINE

"Yup," Paul said, "got fired as soon as Travis got home."

"I'm sorry," Clint said. "Can I buy you a drink to make up for it?"

"You can try," Paul said, "but I don't think one beer is gonna do it."

"Let's give it a try and see how many it will take," Clint suggested.

He called the bartender over and ordered two beers.

"My name's Clint Adams."

"I remember that from this afternoon," Paul said. "Mine's Paul Nicholas."

"Friends call you Paul?"

Paul Nicholas made a face and said, "I prefer Nick."

"Well, since I got you fired, maybe I should call you Paul."

Nicholas actually smiled and said, "Just make it Nick."

When the bartender brought the beers, Clint picked them up and handed one to Nick.

"How long did you have the job?"

"A few months."

"Are you in love with Rachel Hollitt, like every other man in this town?"

Nick smiled.

"I've had my fantasies about her. She's a beautiful girl. But to answer your question, no, I'm not in love with her."

"What will you do now?"

Nick shrugged.

"I got a room at the hotel, and I got enough money to last me a little while. I've got time to decide what my plans should be. Why?"

"Well . . . since you've been fired by the Hollitts I thought you might want to help me out a little."

"How? Oh, I see, you still want to get in to see the old man."

"That's right."

"Well, I don't see how I could help you."

"Maybe you can give me a hint about where I could find him. Does he go riding anywhere? Walking? Anything?"

"Sorry."

"Have you ever even seen him in the time you worked there?"

"Never laid eyes on him."

"Who paid you?"

"Travis, Rachel, or the foreman from the mill."

"Gary Lane?"

"That's him."

"What's he like?"

"He's not tall, but he's big, you know what I mean?"

"I think so."

"And ugly—boy, is he ugly."

"Does he ever see the old man?"

"He hardly comes to the house, so I don't think so."

"How long has he worked for the Hollitts?"

"I don't know. Longer than me, but then everyone there has worked there longer than me."

"What's the talk among the other men?"

Nick held up his empty mug before answering, and Clint had the bartender bring him another.

"Talk about what?"

"Old Man Hollitt."

"What about him?"

"Don't you find it odd that nobody has seen him for two years?"

"That long?" Nick asked. "I had no idea . . ."

"What do you think?"

Nick shrugged.

"So he likes to stay inside. So what?"

"You think he's alive?"

Nick looked at Clint in surprise.

"What?"

"He could be dead, you know, and they're just not letting anyone know about it."

Nick stared at Clint for a few moments and then said, "That's a strange idea."

"But possible."

"Possible, yes, but why?"

"For business purposes," Clint said, and then gave Nick the same theory he had given to Stone.

"Well, if that's the case," Nick said after Clint had finished, "I guess you're out of luck."

"I'd like to know that for a fact, though. If it's true, I'd leave."

"Don't say that too loud," Nick warned.

"Why not?"

"Well, if somebody heard you and told the Hollitts maybe they'd tell you the old man is dead just to get you to leave."

"Good point," Clint said.

"Well, thanks for the beer," Nick said. "I think I'll see if I can get into one of those poker games."

"Good luck. I guess I'll see you around town for a while."

"For a little while longer, yeah," Nick said.

Clint watched the man walk over and sit down at one of the tables and wished he'd gotten somebody a little more knowledgeable fired.

THIRTY

Clint remained at the bar and noticed that the sheriff hadn't moved from his table. In fact, he'd moved into the seat Clint had vacated and was watching the room intently.

"Another beer," Clint said to the bartender, who still hadn't spoken a word to him since his arrival in town. Now he silently set another beer in front of Clint and accepted the money for it. Clint decided that next time he'd make the man ask for the money, just to see if he had a voice.

Clint stood with his back to the bar and also watched the room. Did he believe his own theory, that Anson Hollitt could be dead? He wasn't sure. He was surprised himself the first time he said it out loud with Stone. Now, the second time he'd said it, with Nick, it made more sense to him.

Suddenly his next move came to him, and he knew that Paul Nicholas could help him with it. He looked over at the poker table Nick had sat down at and saw that trouble was brewing already.

"Jesus Christ," one of the other players yelled, throwing down his cards, "the man sits down and wins the first five hands he plays. Don't any of you find that funny?"

"I do," another man said.

"Me, too," said a third man, who was just watching the game.

"What are you saying?" Paul Nicholas asked. "I mean, aside from the fact that you're a bad loser."

The man complaining was seated right across from Nick. The second man was seated on a side of the table where Nick couldn't see his gun hand, but Clint could.

The third man, who was just watching, was standing off to Nick's right, so that Nick couldn't see him and the man across from him at the same time.

Clint looked over at the sheriff, who seemed oblivious to what was going on at the poker table. He was looking somewhere else, peering intently at something.

"I'm sayin' you're a cheater, mister," the first man said.

"If you think that," Nick said, "then get out of the game."

"After losing five hands in a row to you? And you just sat down? How about you leave the game—only leave your money behind, too."

"Not a chance," Nick said.

"Mister, you lookin' to die for money?"

"What if I'm not the one who dies?" Nick asked.

"What if we find out," the other man said, and went for his gun.

Nick upended the table as he came out of his seat, drawing his colt. Clint could see that the man was good with a gun, but there was nothing he could do about the two men he couldn't see. He clearly had the first man beat; he fired once, hitting him in the chest.

"Nick! To your right!" Clint shouted.

Clint drew and shot the other seated man, who was bringing his gun out as he ducked away from the fallen table.

Nick turned to his right in time to see the standing man, and he and Clint fired at the same time, both shots hitting the man.

"Hold it!" Sheriff Cactus Stone shouted when the action was all over.

Paul Nicholas looked over at Clint and saluted him. Clint waved back just as Stone came up next to Nicholas.

"I'll take your gun, mister."

"It was self-defense, Sheriff."

"Sure it was—"

"If you take his gun, you'll have to take mine, too, Cactus," Clint said, moving in on the action.

"What?"

"I killed this one," Clint said, pointing to one of the men on the floor, "and this one."

"I killed this one," Nick said, pointing to the man both he and Clint had killed.

"We both shot him," Clint said, "but my shot killed him."

"My shot killed him."

Stone looked confused.

"They're telling the truth, Sheriff," one of the other players finally spoke up. "That man called this fella a cheater and drew on him. Then these other two drew. This fella," he said, indicating Paul Nicholas, "would have been a goner if it wasn't for . . . for that man." He pointed at Clint.

Most of the people in the saloon were still standing, having jumped for cover when the shooting started.

"All right," Stone said, looking around. "Riley, Bennett, Sacks, get some more men and take these dead men to the undertaker's. Come on. Move! Everybody else just sit down."

There was a lot of movement for a while, while bodies were removed and money was picked up from the floor. The table was righted, and somebody went about seeing to it that each player got his money back.

"What about the money from the two dead men, Cactus?" one of the players asked.

"Split it evenly," Stone said. "They're not gonna need it."

"Well done, Cactus," Clint said.

Stone looked at him and said, "I didn't even know anything was goin' on. I was watching the man at the end of the bar."

Clint turned and looked and didn't see the man anymore.

"Well, it looks like he's gone," Clint said, "so I guess you can stop watching him."

THIRTY-ONE

"Time for me to buy *you* a beer," Nick said when he'd retrieved his money. "You saved my life."

"No argument," Clint said.

They went to the bar and, within minutes of the entire incident, everything was back to normal—except that there were less men in the poker game.

They ordered and soon had a beer each. It was as if they had never moved, never killed three men.

"You did pretty well there," Clint said.

Nick looked at him and said, "I'd be dead if it wasn't for you."

"You've got to widen your range of sight," Clint said. "See everything that's going on around you. Did you know that those two had a friend watching the game?"

"Can't say I did know," Nick admitted.

"Ah," Clint said, "you're young, you'll learn."

"If I stay alive long enough." He finished his beer and got another one. "Okay, so what else can I do to help you?"

"Help me?"

"About Old Man Anson."

"Well," Clint said, "there is one thing."

"What's that?"

"I'd like to know where the mill is."

"That's no problem," Nick said. "In fact, I'll take you there tomorrow."

"There's no need for that," Clint said. "You might be buying yourself a big piece of my trouble."

Nick laughed and said, "Like you didn't just buy yourself a piece of mine?"

"That's different," Clint said. "That was happening right in front of me. There was no way I could watch you be gunned down by three men— one from behind."

"Well, I didn't see anybody else in this place worried about that, did you? No, if you'll have me, Clint, I'd like to ride along with you. After all, I have no immediate plans."

Clint raised his mug and said, "Oh, I'll have you, if you're willing to come."

"There's a lot of men at that mill," Nick said, "and they're all loyal."

"To who?"

"Depends. Some are loyal to the old man, even though they haven't seen him in a long time. Others are loyal to Travis because he's the one they see every day. Others still are loyal to Lane, because he's been the foreman out there for a long time."

"How does he feel about working for the old man's son?" Clint asked.

"There were some problems in the beginning, I heard, but since I've been here they get along great. In fact, I think they're good friends."

Clint looked around, but Travis Hollitt's other good friend, Sheriff Cactus Stone, had left.

"I wonder if Travis treats all his friends the same," Clint said.

"You mean Cactus?"

"That's who I mean."

"Cactus is a joke around the Hollitt place, Clint."

"Why?"

"Because he thinks he's Travis's friend, and he thinks he's going to marry Rachel."

"And?"

"And neither one of those things is true. Everybody who works there knows it."

"And he's not a very good sheriff, either," Clint said.

"Still, the Hollitts have a man with a badge who will listen to them. That always comes in handy, doesn't it?"

"Yeah," Clint said, remembering other reasons he had stopped wearing a badge, "a lot of people think so."

THIRTY-TWO

Early the next morning Clint and Paul Nicholas were to meet for breakfast. Clint chose the café that Cactus Stone had shown him. As he left the hotel, he saw Sheriff Stone coming across the street toward the hotel.

"Not coming to see me, I hope," he said.

"Yes, I am."

"What now, Cactus?"

"Are you leaving today?"

"I haven't changed my mind since last night."

"You killed a man last night."

"Two," Clint said, and started walking toward the café. Stone walked along with him.

"I can't allow that in this town," Stone said. "I'm the law."

"I know that, Cactus."

"I don't want there to be any more trouble."

"Neither do I."

"What are you gonna do today?"

Clint stopped so abruptly that Stone went on two more steps before he could stop himself.

"We talked about this yesterday, Cactus. Nothing's changed. I'm still not leaving until I see Old Man Hollitt. That's final."

"You're pretty damned stubborn, you know that?"

"So I've been told. I'm going to have breakfast with a friend now. Is that all right with you?"

"Long as you don't kill him," Stone groused.

"Cactus," Clint said, in mock surprise, "you have a sense of humor."

He left Cactus Stone standing with his hands on his hips, exasperation plain on his face.

"What's wrong?" Paul Nicholas asked as Clint walked into the café and sat down.

"Oh, nothing. It's just Cactus Stone."

"The sheriff?"

Clint nodded.

"He shouldn't be a problem."

"I feel sorry for him," Clint said. "He's not cut out to be a lawman, and sooner or later he's going to find that out . . . probably the hard way."

"That's his problem."

"I guess so."

Clint looked across at the man he now knew as Nick and realized that he was a bit older than he'd originally guessed.

"How old are you? Twenty-five? Twenty-six?"

"Twenty-eight," Nick said, "but who's counting. I know, I look younger, but it'll catch up to me."

"What will?"

Nick grinned.

"The hard living. I'll look my age in no time."

Clint decided to get down to business.

"How long a ride is it to the mill?"

"Half an hour, maybe a little more."

"Will Travis be there this early?"

"Probably not."

"And Lane?"

"He'll be there, definitely. You plan on talking to him?"

"I don't know what I plan to do," Clint admitted honestly. "I just want to see where the mill is. The two things people have been trying to keep from me since I got here are the location of the house and the location of the mill. I just want to know those things, and then I'll figure out my next move."

They ordered breakfast and ate it quickly.

"Can you tell me something, Clint?"

"What?"

"Do you mean the old man any harm?"

"Why?"

Nick shrugged.

"I'd just like to know."

"No, I don't mean anybody any harm. I've been saying that since I got here, too, but nobody believes me."

"I believe you."

"Thanks."

They finished breakfast and walked to the livery for their horses.

"I can pay you for your time," Clint said while they were saddling the animals.

Nick didn't answer.

"You insulted?"

"I'm trying to decide," Nick said, "whether or not I should accept."

"I did cost you your job."

"No, you didn't," he said. "I did. If I wanted to keep it so bad, I should have shot you."

"Well," Clint said, "I guess I should be glad you didn't want to keep your job that bad."

"That's what it comes down to."

They mounted up and headed out of the livery.

"I'll take you up on it."

"On what?" Clint asked.

"Paying me."

"How much?"

Nick made a show of thinking it over.

"Cover my food," he said, "and pay for my hotel."

"Okay."

"And drinks."

"Okay."

They rode in silence to the end of town.

"That it?" Clint asked.

"That's it."

"Then we've got a deal."

"The mill's that way." Nick pointed in a general direction.

"Lead on, then."

THIRTY-THREE

Gary Lane was standing at the window of the office when he saw the two riders coming. One he recognized from the house. Since he was up-to-date on everything that was happening, he knew that Paul Nicholas had been fired yesterday. He also knew why.

Lane walked over to the desk, took out a little .32 Colt, and tucked it into his belt. His jacket would keep it from showing.

He opened the door and stepped out to wait.

"That's Lane."

Clint looked up at the office, the front of which was on stilts. The back of it was on the mountain slope. The man coming out was very thick and built low to the ground. From this angle it looked like he had no neck. Clint couldn't see his face, so he couldn't tell whether or not he was truly ugly.

They reined their horses in.

"He's waiting for us," Nick said.

"I can see that."

"You want to talk to him?"

"About what?"

"Old Man Hollitt. Maybe he knows whether he's dead or not."

"Maybe he does," Clint said thoughtfully. "Okay, let's talk to him."

"Chances are he's got a gun under his jacket."

"How do you know that?"

"I heard some of the others talk."

"Thanks for the warning."

"He'll also know that I've been fired."

"How do you know that?"

Nick looked at Clint.

"He knows everything that goes on here or at the house."

"I'll do the talking then."

"Fine," Nick said. "I never liked talking to him anyway."

They continued on. As they approached the office, Lane started down the steps to meet them. Around them men stopped what they were doing to watch.

"Good morning," Clint greeted.

Up close he saw that Gary Lane truly was an ugly man. His face looked mashed and misshapen, but his eyes were intelligent.

"I thought you got fired, Nicholas," Lane said, ignoring Clint.

"I did."

"What are you doing here?"

"He works for me now."

Lane looked at Clint.

"As what?"

"A guide."

Lane frowned.

"You're Adams."

"That's right."

"What do you want?"

"Just to talk."

"About what?"

"The Hollitts."

"They're a good family."

"So I hear."

"If you mean to hurt them, you've got an enemy in me."

"Why does everyone assume I mean to hurt them?"

"You tell me."

"What are your instructions about me?"

"I don't have any. I make up my own mind."

"Why are you talking to me?"

"You're here. It would be rude of me not to."

"Will you talk about the family?"

"No."

"About Leonard Hollitt?"

"No."

"About the mill?"

"No."

"How about Travis and Rachel?"

"No."

"What will you talk about?"

"The weather."

"It's cold."

"You need a jacket."

"I'm starting to think so."

"Preferably fur-lined."

"Like yours?"

"Yes."

"It hides the gun well."

"I can still get to it if I have to."

"You won't have to."

"Can I help you with anything else?"

"You've just about ruled out everything but the weather, and I don't need any help with that. I think we'll be going."

"Don't come back."

"Why not?"

"It wouldn't be healthy."

Clint stared at Lane and saw in the man's eyes that he was dangerous.

"I'll keep that in mind."

He turned Duke and started away, with Nick close behind. After they'd ridden a short ways he turned in his saddle and saw that Lane was still watching them.

"He's a scary man," Nick said.

"I can see that."

"And he's fiercely loyal."

Clint turned and they rode on.

"To who?"

"What?"

"Loyal to who? The old man? Travis?"

Nick took a moment to think that one over.

"From what I heard when I first came to work here, I would have thought he was loyal to the old man, but lately he and Travis have been real close."

"So you think Lane would do whatever Travis asked him, no matter what?"

"What are you thinking?"

"I'm still thinking about the old man being dead."

"Being dead?" Nick asked. "Or being killed?"

Clint didn't answer.

"You really think Travis would kill his own father to take control of the company?"

"It's been done before."

"It would have to be done without Rachel," Nick said, "and I don't think that's possible. If the old man is dead and they're not letting anyone know, Rachel would have to be in on that. She'd never go along if she thought they killed him."

"What if she doesn't know?"

"I don't know," Nick said. "I never even got a whiff of that kind of thing, Clint."

"Who goes in the house?"

"Just Travis and Rachel."

"Nobody else?"

"Just Martha, the cook. I've never seen anyone else go into the house . . . except . . ."

"Except who?"

"Well, I saw Lane go in, but that was only once."

"When?"

"Oh, don't know . . . a couple of months ago."

"You know what we need?"

"What?"

"We need to talk to somebody who has worked

there a lot longer than you."

"Nobody's going to talk against the Hollitts, Clint."

"Maybe they will," Clint said, "if they don't realize they're doing it."

THIRTY-FOUR

By the time they got back to town, Nick had narrowed the field down to three men.

"Hal Teacher has worked there the longest of anyone I know," he said as they rode to the livery.

"How old is he?"

"I don't know . . . sixty, maybe."

"So he worked for Old Man Hollitt way back when."

"I guess so."

"Why do you think he'd talk?"

"Because he does."

"What?"

"It's all he does, talk, talk, talk. Nobody wants to work with him, or go to town with him, because he chews their ears off."

"So all we'd have to do is listen to him."

"Right."

"Does he always make sense?"

"That's another thing. He rambles . . . a lot."

"Well, who else is there?"

As they dismounted in front of the livery, Nick said, "Dave Kendall."

"What's his story?"

They walked their horses inside and started to unsaddle them.

"He thinks he should have Gary Lane's job."

"So he's unhappy?"

"Oh, yeah."

"Why does he stay?"

"Because he still thinks that someday he'll get it."

"Why would he talk?"

"He complains," Nick said, "he just loves to complain."

They finished settling their animals in and left the livery.

"Saloon?" Nick asked.

"Why not?"

"You're buying."

"I remember."

They walked to the saloon, got a couple of beers. It was early and there was only one other man in the place besides the bartender.

"Have you ever heard him talk?" Clint asked.

"Who?"

"The bartender."

"Sure, why?"

"I thought maybe he was mute. He's never said a word to me."

"Maybe he's just got nothing to say."

"Maybe."

They went to a back table and sat down.

"Okay, who's the third man?" Clint asked.

"His name's Billy McBride. He's about thirty, and he's in love with Rachel."

"The way I hear it, who isn't?"

"No," Nick said, "I mean he's *really* in love with her. He doesn't just have a crush on her, or lust after her, he loves her."

"Like Cactus?"

"No," Nick said, "Cactus loves her and wants to marry her."

"So how is that different from Billy?"

"Billy *loves* her," Nick said. "How can I put this? He . . . worships her. He thinks she's . . ."

"A goddess?"

"That's it," Nick said. "A goddess. He thinks the sun rises and sets with her."

"So he's crazy about her."

"So crazy it's made him crazy. He thinks it's his lot in life to keep her safe and unharmed."

"So why would he talk?"

Nick shrugged.

"If he thought something was going on that would hurt her, I think he'd talk plenty."

"If he has anything to say."

"Well, he might."

"What's that mean?"

"He spends a lot of time up at the house."

"I thought nobody went inside?"

"I don't mean inside."

Clint waited, then said, "Well, what do you mean, Nick?"

"He goes up there and . . . looks in the windows."

"He spies on Rachel?"

Nick nodded.

"A lot?"

"Every night."

"So if anything was going on in the house he might know about it."

"He might."

"And do all three of these men come to town?"

"They do."

"You know what?"

"What?"

"I think we should talk to all three of them. Are you friends with them?"

"Not exactly. I mean, I didn't make a lot of real friends while I worked there, but we're on friendly terms. I mean, I talk to them, they talk to me."

"What are you saying?"

"I'm not sure if they'll talk to me or not."

"Well," Clint said, "we'll just have to see about that."

THIRTY-FIVE

The first one they talked to was the old man, Hal Teacher. He came into town in the late afternoon and headed right for the saloon. Clint and Nick were sitting at a table in the back.

"That's him," Nick said.

"Invite him over."

Nick got up and walked to the bar before Teacher had a chance to pay for his drink. Clint watched as Nick spoke to Teacher, and then both men came walking over. Nick was carrying Teacher's beer.

" . . . tough that you got fired like that," the old man was saying. "Was it really because you wouldn't shoot somebody?"

"It was," Clint said, "and I'm the somebody."

The old man looked at him and asked, "You're Clint Adams?"

"That's right."

Teacher sat down across from Clint. Nick put

141

his beer in front of him and sat down himself.

"So you're the Gunsmith, huh?"

"That's right."

"You're causin' a lot of commotion up at the main house."

"Is that right?"

"Young Travis is ready to have your head blown off."

"Has he got the men who can do it?"

The old man blew some air out his mouth and then drank some beer.

"We're lumbermen, some of us are ranch hands, but none of us are gunmen. I think you're safe for now."

They talked about the lumber business for a while, and Nick got up and down a few times to bring the old man fresh drinks. Teacher was into his fourth beer when he started talking about Anson Hollitt, and Travis.

"What's Travis so worried about, anyway?" Clint asked.

"You'd know that better than me, mister."

"All I'm trying to do is talk with Anson Hollitt."

"Good luck," Teacher said. "Nobody has seen Anson in years."

"Not even you?"

Teacher squinted over the edge of his beer mug.

"Why should I see him?"

"You've worked for him for a long time."

"So?"

"Can you work for a man that long and not become friends?"

"Apparently you can," Teacher said, and he

didn't look happy. "You know, there was a time when I thought me and Anson was friends—a long time, but that changed."

"What changed it?"

"His wife died."

"When was that?"

"Few years back," Teacher said. "He changed then."

"How?"

"Stayed in the house, never came out, let young Travis handle everything."

"Including Leonard?"

"Who?"

"Leonard Hollitt?"

Teacher stared at Clint for a few moments, then said, "Never heard of 'im."

"Sure you have, Mr. Teacher," Clint said. "He was Anson's bastard."

Teacher remained silent for a time, then said, "Maybe he was, but Travis took care of that, too."

"How'd he do that?"

"Same way the rich always do it."

"Ah," Clint said, "with money."

"You bet, with money. Paid that young man off, and away he went."

But not happily, Clint thought. The money could only last so long and then you started thinking again about having no family. You started thinking about being denied by a father who didn't want you.

"I wonder who the mother was," Clint said.

Suddenly, it was as if Teacher sobered up and realized he'd been talking. He pushed his chair back and staggered to his feet.

"Gotta go."

"So soon?" Clint asked.

"Gotta go," he said again. Then he held his finger to his lips and added, "Don't tell nobody I talked to you . . ."

As if everyone in the saloon hadn't already seen them together.

"Gotta go," Teacher said, and rushed from the saloon.

"That's one," Clint said to Nick.

THIRTY-SIX

Dave Kendall came to town a little bit later in the evening. Clint and Nick were still sitting in the saloon when he walked in.

"There's Kendall."

"Okay," Clint said, "invite him over."

Once again Nick went to the bar and came back with a man and a beer.

"What's this all about?" Kendall asked. He was a barrel-chested man in his forties with a perpetual scowl on his face. "Are you really Clint Adams?"

"That's right."

Kendall sat down, but he did so warily. Nick put his beer in front of him and also sat.

"I could get fired for talking to you," Kendall said, looking around. "Look what happened to Paul, here."

"I know," Clint said. "Listen, you're free to

go, if you like. I just thought we'd buy you a beer."

"What for?"

"Why not?"

"I don't know you."

"You know Paul."

"Yeah, but we ain't friends."

"Do you have a lot of friends, Mr. Kendall?"

"What's that got to do with anything?"

"I guess if you were foreman of the mill, you'd have lots of friends."

Kendall frowned.

"What do you know about that?"

"Only that you think you should be foreman."

"I don't think, I know."

"Then why aren't you?"

"Because the old man don't think I should be."

"I thought Travis ran the business?"

"Travis don't run nothin'," Kendall said, "and neither does Lane."

"Who does, then?" Clint asked.

"The old man."

"I thought he was dead."

"What?" Kendall looked shocked.

"That's what I heard."

"I don't know where you heard it, but that's crazy," Kendall said. "Maybe nobody's seen him, but he's runnin' the show from inside the house."

"You know that for a fact?"

Kendall hadn't touched his beer yet, and now he looked down at it.

"I shouldn't be talkin' to you," he said. "It could cost me my job."

"Like I said," Clint replied, "that's up to you."

Kendall pushed his chair back and stood up.

"I'll buy my own beer, too."

As Kendall walked away from them, Nick said, "Didn't get much there."

"Maybe he grouses about not being foreman," Clint said, "but that man is loyal to Anson Hollitt."

"So where does that leave us?"

"We've got one man left, don't we?"

"Yeah, but I doubt he'll be in town tonight."

"Why?"

"Kendall, and even old Teach, they come in, have a few drinks, and then go over to the whorehouse."

"But not Billy?"

"Billy hasn't been with a woman since he first laid eyes on Rachel," Nick said. "Now, I think Rachel's a beautiful woman, but that's a long time to go without."

"So how do we get to talk to Billy?"

"We either find him at work, or find him following Rachel."

"He follows her?"

Nick nodded.

"This boy's got it bad, huh?"

"The worst."

"Well, if you're right and he doesn't show up, I guess we'll have to go looking for him tomorrow."

"We spend the rest of the night in here?"

"We do."

"How about some poker?"

"Not for me," Clint said. "I remember what happened the last time."

"Oh," Nick said, "right. I guess it's time for another beer, then."

THIRTY-SEVEN

Billy McBride did not come into town that night, so when it got late enough to quit waiting Clint announced he was going to his hotel.

"I'm going to stay around here awhile longer," Nick said. "I'm trying to decide between the little redhead and the big dark-haired woman."

"Take the big one," Clint said.

"Why?"

"The little one has too much energy. She'll keep you up all night."

"You speaking from personal experience?"

"Yes," Clint said, "but not with her, specifically, just with women like her."

"I'll keep it in mind."

Clint left the saloon and started walking up the street toward his hotel. As he passed the alley next to the saloon, he heard something and turned his head. The move saved his life. An axe handle came down and would have struck him on the head if he hadn't turned. Instead it hit him on the point of the right shoulder. He cried out and his right arm went dead.

He staggered away from the alley into the street, pursued by three dark figures. He couldn't draw his gun right-handed because that arm was deadened completely.

They all had axe handles and apparently their intent was to beat him to death. He knew he couldn't wait for them to start swinging again. He would only be able to defend himself with his left arm, and if that one was damaged he would be defenseless.

He kept moving away from them, knowing that he had to draw his gun left-handed if he had any chance of staying alive. They closed in on him and started to swing, and he went down to the ground, rolling himself up to protect his left arm. As blows rained down on him, he reached across his body, drew his gun left-handed, and fired at someone's leg. At that moment he was struck a blow on the head that made his ears ring and his vision swirl. Convulsively, he pulled the trigger again. . . .

There was a cry of pain and suddenly they weren't hitting him anymore. Somebody yelled from what seemed to be far away and then there were more shots. He may have fired again, but he wasn't sure because his head was still swimming. . . .

Clint was sitting on an examining table in the doctor's office. Dr. Theodore Martin was examining the welts on his back and maneuvering his right arm around.

"I don't think the shoulder is broken, but it's going to be sore for a while. These welts on his back will hurt, too, but he was wise to roll up the way he did. Those axe handles could have crushed his ribs."

"How's his head, Doc?" Nick asked.

"He's cut, but not badly."

"I wish the two of you would stop talking about me like I'm not here."

"Sorry," Nick said.

"You can get dressed," the doctor said. "There's no permanent damage."

"Thanks, Doc."

"Are you staying at the hotel?"

"Yes."

"I'll send you my bill." He was a gray-haired man who probably looked distinguished when dressed. At the moment he was wearing an old bathrobe. "Right now I'm going back to bed. I don't stay up till all hours like you youngsters."

"Thanks again, Doc."

When Clint was dressed, Nick said, "The sheriff wants us to come over to his office when you're finished here."

"Well, let's go, then," Clint said, "but let's go slow . . ."

They walked over to the sheriff's office with Clint moving very slowly. His shoulder was the worse thing because the axe handle had hit him right on the point. His arm still didn't have all of the feeling back in it.

"Did you see who they were?" Nick asked.

"Not at the time," Clint said. "I was too busy covering up. How about you?"

"They were running when I got outside."

"What about the one you killed?"

"I still haven't seen him. I guess Cactus will tell us who he is."

When they entered the sheriff's office, Stone wasn't there yet. Clint sat down in front of Stone's desk and Nick leaned against it.

"Probably still at the undertaker's," Nick said.

"I wonder if the one you killed is the one I shot in the leg. If not, we might be able to find him."

"Limping around town?"

"Nah," Clint said, "he'll find a hole someplace now."

Nick looked at Clint.

"You think Travis Hollitt sent them, don't you?"

"Who else? Do you think they were out to rob me?"

"Well, if they're men from the mill I'll recognize them, and so will Cactus."

At that moment the door opened and Sheriff Cactus Stone entered.

"You told me there wouldn't be no more trouble," he said accusingly to Clint.

"Cactus," Clint said, "they came after me with axe handles. What was I supposed to do? Besides, I just shot one in the leg."

"There's a dead man at the undertaker's."

"I killed him," Nick said. "When I came out of the saloon, I saw them running away and I fired."

"Why?"

Nick shrugged.

"It seemed the thing to do at the time."

Stone walked around his desk and sat down.

"So?" Clint asked.

"So what?"

"Who was it?"

Stone frowned.

"You know him, don't you?"

No answer.

"He works for the Hollitts," Clint said. "At least, he does tonight. Tomorrow they'll probably claim that they fired him."

"A lot of that going around," Nick said.

"Who was it, Cactus?"

"His name was Billy McBride."

Clint and Nick exchanged a glance.

THIRTY-EIGHT

Clint was in bed the next morning when there was a knock on his door. He started to get up but stopped short when the pain hit. His back hurt in several places, and his shoulder was on fire.

The knocking on the door persisted, and he finally dragged himself out of bed to open it.

"You killed one of my men!" Travis Hollitt shouted.

Clint walked back and sat down on the bed. Shouting was not the most aggressive thing Hollitt could have done, and the fact that he chose to shout told Clint something.

"Three of your men attacked me," Clint said, "probably by your order. I shot one, and one was killed by someone else. The sheriff has the whole story."

"I'm warning you, Adams," Hollitt said, "if you don't leave town, the next dead man will be you."

"Hollitt," Clint said, "if I were you, I'd get out of here right now."

"Oh, yeah? Why?"

"Because as sore and stiff as I am, if you don't leave I'll throw you out myself—out the window!"

Travis Hollitt stared at Clint, clearly unsure as to what to do next. Clint knew now that Hollitt was personally capable of very little beyond some shouting. If he was able to do more, he would have by now.

"Get out," Clint said, "and tell your father to expect me today."

"You can't—"

"Today," Clint said again. "I'm through fooling around with you and your family. I'm going to do what I came to do today and get out of here."

Hollitt stood there and stared at Clint, who then pushed himself painfully to his feet. He didn't have to take a step, though, because Hollitt chose that moment to turn and leave. Clint closed the door, then staggered back to the bed to lie down.

The next knock on the door was less insistent.

"Clint? It's Nick. You okay?"

"Give me a minute."

Once again, for the second time in an hour, Clint managed to stand up and move to the door. After he opened it he immediately backed up and sat down on the bed.

"I thought you might need some help," Nick said.

"Only walking, dressing, and breathing."

"That bad?"

"Maybe not."

Clint stood up and walked to the basin and pitcher on top of the dresser. As Clint poured water, Nick took a deep breath. Clint's back was a mass of crisscrossing welts and bruises.

"Nice color on your back."

"The doctor said I'd be stiff when I woke up," Clint said. "He was right. He also said I'd loosen up as the day went along. We'll have to see how right he is about that as we go along."

Clint washed himself and then reached for his clothes.

"Want help?"

He shook his head. Dressing was a slow, painful process but he finally managed it on his own.

"What do you want to do first?" Nick said.

"Breakfast."

It even hurt to talk, so for a while his answers to questions would be short ones.

"And after that?"

"I'll tell you later. Let's go downstairs and eat right here in the hotel."

"Okay," Nick said. "Want help?"

"Just walk ahead of me on the stairs in case I fall," Clint said. "Other than that I want to be on my own."

"Okay," Nick said. "You're calling the shots."

"Why's that?"

Nick shrugged and said, "You're the one who got beat up."

"Next time," Clint said, "you can call the shots."

THIRTY-NINE

"It wasn't a smart thing to do, Travis," Stone said.

"For the last time," Hollitt said, "I didn't send anyone after Adams."

"The dead man's one of yours, right?"

"McBride, right."

"You didn't fire him?"

"Why would I fire him?"

"I don't know," Stone said, "you've already fired one man this week."

"That was Rachel's doing. She wanted him off the property."

"So if you didn't send those men after Adams, who did?" Stone asked.

"I don't know."

"Lane?"

"Maybe."

"What about Rachel?"

Hollitt made a face.

"I'll ask her."

"How about your father?"

"No," Hollitt said, "he didn't do it."

"How can you be sure? Did you ask him?"

"Trust me on this, Cactus," Hollitt said. "He didn't do it."

"Well, then, you better talk to Lane and Rachel and see who did, and tell them not to do it again."

"I'll talk to them," Hollitt said, shaking his head and moving toward the door. "Hey, Cactus?"

"Yeah."

"You're startin' to sound like a real sheriff."

"Thanks, Travis."

"I didn't say I liked it," Hollitt said and left.

Well, whether Travis Hollitt liked it or not, Cactus Stone was starting to feel like a real sheriff. It must have had something to do with talking to Clint Adams. All of a sudden Stone was feeling like he didn't want anybody else dying in his town. He had never thought of Winter Creek as his town before, but he was thinking that way now.

It was time to talk to Clint Adams again. As much as he liked learning from the man, the trouble had started when he first came to town. Stone wanted to find out what Clint Adams was planning to do next.

FORTY

Over breakfast Clint told Nick about Travis Hollitt coming to see him.

"You told him what?"

"That I'd be out to see his father today."

"Why didn't he just kill you?"

"It's not in him."

"Huh?"

"How well do you know Travis, Nick?"

"Not well."

"I saw something in him today I hadn't seen before."

"What?"

"He's not capable of much more than threatening and yelling. The nastier stuff he must leave to other people."

"So you don't think he sent those men after you?"

"No."

"Who then? Lane?"

"You tell me."

Nick thought a minute.

"Naw."

"Why not?"

"Lane would have come to town and taken care of you himself."

"Well," Clint said, "I guess that only leaves one person."

"Who?"

"Rachel."

Nick laughed, then stopped.

"Rachel sent those men after you?"

"That's the way I see it. You said yourself McBride was crazy about her. I bet she approached him, and he lined up the other two men. Would he do that for her?"

"I think he would have done anything for her."

"Well, that's it, then."

"So what now?"

"I still intend to go and see Old Man Hollitt today," Clint said. "I want to do what I came here to do and get out of this town."

"When you leave would you mind some company?"

"I have to head back to Dawson City."

"I'll just ride along for a while, until I decide what I want to do."

Clint shrugged.

"It's all right with me."

"Good. Thanks. Uh, are you gonna be able to ride a horse today?"

"I don't know," Clint said. "First I've got to see if I can get up from this chair."

• • •

During the ride back to the mill, Travis Hollitt decided that it could only have been Gary Lane who'd sent those men to town. It was Lane's style. When he got there, he accused the foreman.

"I don't get this," Lane said.

"What?"

"You don't know that's not my style? How long have we known each other?"

"It's violence, Gary," Hollitt said, "and you're more violent than I am."

"Maybe so," Lane said, "but I wouldn't send anybody to do my fighting for me—especially not three incompetents. Who got killed?"

"McBride."

"Well, there you go."

"What?"

"McBride's in love with Rachel."

"So?"

"He'd do anything she asked."

For a moment Hollitt just stared at him.

"You're accusing Rachel—"

"Who else? Did you do it?"

"No."

"Well, neither did I."

Travis Hollitt thought about it again, then scratched his head and said, "Son of a bitch."

"You better have a talk with her, Travis," Lane said, "before she does something even dumber."

"I better get to the house," Hollitt said, and left the office.

Eventually Clint was able to make it out of the chair and out of the hotel.

"I want to walk awhile," he said to Nick. "Maybe that'll loosen me up."

"It's worth a try, I guess. We just better hope that nobody else makes a try for you while you're in this condition."

"Maybe," Clint said, as they walked, "I should go out and talk to Rachel before she picks out three or four more men for the job."

"We might as well walk toward the livery, then," Nick said. "I'll saddle your horse for you and ride out there with you."

Clint looked at Nick, who hastily added, "Just in case you fall off your horse along the way."

FORTY-ONE

Travis Hollitt got to the house before Clint Adams and Paul Nicholas did.

"Nobody gets through that gate without my okay, understand?" he said to the man on the gate.

"Yessir."

"My okay, and mine only!"

"Yessir."

He rode up to the house, dismounted, and went up the steps without worrying about the horse.

"Rachel!" he shouted as he entered.

They had one servant, the cook, a woman named Martha who had been with the family for years. She came out of the kitchen and through the dining room, wiping her hands on her apron.

"Martha, is my sister home?"

"Yes, sir," the old woman said. "She said she'd be upstairs in your father's room."

"Thank you."

"She took him some soup," Martha said. Then she shouted up the steps after him, "I swear, that man doesn't eat enough to keep a bird alive."

Travis walked down the hall to the door to his father's room and entered without knocking. Rachel was sitting in a chair opposite her father's bed, staring at it. The bowl of soup was cooling on a table next to the bed.

"He might as well be dead," she said, staring at the still form lying in the bed.

"Rachel, we have to talk."

"When will people start to suspect?" she wondered out loud. Her brother did not think she was talking to him, but to herself.

"Rachel!"

Startled, she looked up at her brother.

"I'm waiting for the soup to cool, otherwise it dribbles down his chin."

"Why did you send McBride and two other men after Clint Adams last night?"

"Did they kill him?"

"No—"

"Hurt him?"

"Not seriously."

"Well, maybe it will scare him away."

"You don't scare away a man like Clint Adams, not with violence."

"But that's the way he lives, isn't it? By violence? What else would you use, Travis?"

"We have to use our heads, Rachel."

She turned to stare at her father again.

"Are we doing the right thing, Travis? Hiding this from people?"

"We've already discussed this, Rachel. If word gets out that Pa is in this condition we'll lose business."

"But . . . he hasn't even been seen by a doctor. How do we know a doctor wouldn't be able to cure this?"

"We can't take the chance that a doctor would see him and then talk. Don't you see? We'd lose everything."

"That's why I sent those men after Clint Adams," she said, looking at her brother again, "so that you wouldn't lose everything."

"Not me, Rachel," Travis Hollitt said, "we, both of us."

She shook her head.

"I have nothing to lose, Travis. The business is yours, not mine." She looked at the man in the bed and said, "I simply want my father back."

Travis did something he hadn't done since entering the room. He looked at his father— that is, at the figure in the bed that once was his father. The man had lost so much weight he barely seemed to be there beneath the bedclothes.

The truth of the matter was that he didn't want his father back. Now that he was running the business, he liked it. The best thing for all of them would be if the man just wasted away and died.

"Rachel, you have to promise me that you won't do anything foolish again," he said. "You've got to let me handle this. Agreed?"

She didn't answer.

"Rachel!"

"All right," she snapped. "I agree."

"Good," Hollitt said, feeling better. "I have to go back to the mill." He hesitated, then added, "Take care of him."

"I do," she said. As her brother left the room she added, "It's all I do."

FORTY-TWO

"This isn't going to be easy," Clint said. Today Duke looked bigger and higher than he'd ever looked before.

"Maybe we need to wait another day," Nick suggested.

"No," Clint said, "I want to confront Rachel with what happened last night. I don't want her to have too much time to think about it."

"Maybe she hasn't heard yet what happened."

"I'm sure her brother has told her by now," Clint said, "and maybe even chastised her. Let's try this again."

He slid his foot into the stirrup, grabbed hold of the pommel of the saddle, and heaved. The pain went through his shoulder and his back—and then suddenly Nick put his hands against Clint's butt and pushed and he was in the saddle.

"There ya go," Nick said.

Clint stared down at the man, waiting for his muscles to stop protesting, and said, "Thanks."

Nick walked around and mounted his own horse, and they started out at a pace Clint could take.

They were getting close to the house when Nick said, "There's gonna be a man on the gate, you know."

"I know."

"How do we get past him?"

"We could ask."

"What if he's not like me? What if he shoots you on sight?"

"Will he shoot you on sight?"

"I don't think so," Nick said, "but why do I tell him I'm here?"

Clint thought a moment, then said, "Back pay?"

Nick considered it for a moment, then nodded and said, "That could work."

They decided that they would ride up to the gate together, but that Nick would do the talking.

"Do you know him?" Clint asked as they approached the gate.

"Looks like Jack Coulson."

When they reached the gate, Nick said, "Hi, Jack."

"Hey, Nicholas." The man looked at him from between the bars of the metal gate. "What are you doin' here?"

"I came for my back pay, Jack."

"Well, Travis left. He went to the mill."

"I'm supposed to see Miss Hollitt."

"Yeah," Coulson said, "wouldn't we all like to?"

"Come on, open up the gate, will you?"

Coulson frowned.

"Who's he?"

"Just a friend of mine."

"He can't come in."

"I told you, he's just a friend of mine."

"You don't even work here anymore, Nicholas," Coulson said. "Just wait there while I check with the house—"

Nick drew his gun and pointed it at the man.

"Drop the rifle, Jack."

"What's goin' on?"

"Just do as he says." Although Clint might not have gone about getting the gate open this way, it certainly looked as if it was going to work.

"You wouldn't shoot me, Nick," Coulson said.

"He might not," Clint said, drawing his own gun, "but I will. Now open the gate."

Coulson tossed the rifle aside, unlocked the gate, and opened it. Clint and Nick rode through. They made Coulson close it and lock it after him, and then stand aside.

"What's going to happen when we're seen riding up to the house?" Clint asked Nick.

"They'll assume we were let in. What do we do with him?"

Coulson was standing there with his hands up.

"We just need him out of the way for a little while. We might as well tie him up."

Nick turned and struck the man on the head with his gun. Coulson slumped to the ground, falling back out of sight of the gate.

Nick looked at Clint and said, "Next best thing."

FORTY-THREE

They rode slowly to the house, and Nick actually nodded and said hello to a couple of men. Nobody attempted to stop or challenge them.

When they reached the house, they dismounted—Clint very carefully—and left their horses right out front. They mounted the steps to the front door and knocked.

"Try it," Clint said.

Nick tried the door. It was locked. They knocked again.

The door was opened by an elderly woman who frowned at them.

"Hello, Martha," Nick said. "I'm Paul Nicholas. Remember?"

"You don't work here anymore," she said.

"Is Miss Hollitt home?" Clint asked.

"Who are you?"

"I'm the man asking if Miss Hollitt is home."

"I don't know you—"

"Excuse me," Clint said, and slipped by the woman, barely brushing her.

"You can't go in there," she said, but she did nothing to try to physically stop him. She couldn't have.

Nick entered after him.

"First time I've been in here," he said. "It's nice."

"Look around down here," Clint said.

"Right."

They split up and covered the downstairs, then met back in the entry foyer again.

"Nothing," Nick said.

"She must be upstairs," Clint said. "If the old man is sick, that's where he'd be."

"And if he's dead?" Nick asked.

"Who knows where he'd be? Let's try the upstairs."

"Right."

"You can't—" Martha started, but she saw there was no use.

Suddenly, Rachel Hollitt appeared at the top of the stairs, holding a gun.

"What are you doing in this house?" she demanded.

The staircase was wide and Clint instinctively moved away from Nick so that they'd present two distinctly separate targets.

"I came to see your father, Rachel."

"They should have killed you last night."

"But they didn't. Will you do it now?"

"If you don't leave, I will." Clint noticed that the hand holding the gun was shaking.

"I don't think you will, Rachel."

"I swear I will."

"Even if you pulled the trigger," Clint said, moving up another step, "I think you'd miss."

"Why did you have to come here?"

Another step.

"Something's going on here, Rachel and I think you'd like to see it end."

Step.

"It's been very hard on you, hasn't it, keeping it a secret all this time?"

Step.

"And what about Leonard Hollitt?"

"What about him?"

"You didn't know you had another brother, did you? A half brother?"

"What?"

Another step and he was almost within reach of the gun she was holding out.

"Didn't Travis tell you that Leonard was a half brother?"

"You're crazy."

"Ask him. If you think I'm crazy ask Travis . . . or better yet, ask your father."

At the mention of her father she instinctively looked away down the hall toward his room. In that moment Clint snatched the gun from her hand, but she didn't even seem to notice.

"Where is he, Rachel? Where's your father?"

"He's . . . he's in his room."

"Show me."

She turned and walked down the hall. Clint followed, and Nick brought up the rear.

When they reached the bedroom of Anson

Hollitt, Rachel went in first. As Clint entered, the odor hit him. He'd smelled it many places before, usually hospitals and sick rooms.

The smell of death.

The man in the bed was small and frail, and still. On the table next to the bed was a bowl of soup.

"That's him?" Nick asked in a whisper.

"I don't think you have to whisper, Nick," Clint said. "He's not going to hear you."

"You mean . . . he's . . ."

"Dead," Clint said.

"No," Rachel said. "I have to give him his soup."

Clint walked to the bed and touched the man's face. It was cold.

"He's been dead awhile."

"He can't be dead," Rachel said, moving to her father's bedside. "He can't be."

Clint took the letter from Leonard Hollitt out of his pocket and set it down on the dead man's bed, near his right hand.

"Come on," he said to Nick, "I'm done here."

FORTY-FOUR

Much later in the day they were sitting in Sheriff Cactus Stone's office.

"Doc says Mr. Hollitt's been dead a couple of days. Any more and the body would have started to smell."

"That makes sense," Clint said.

"He also says Mr. Hollitt's been in that bed a long time. He's got the bedsores to prove it."

"So the old man's been lying there who knows how long," Clint said, "and Travis has been running the business."

"Do you think they even knew he'd died a couple of days ago?" Nick asked.

"It's scary to think maybe they didn't," Stone said, shivering.

"I wonder what Travis is gonna do when he finds out the body's at the undertaker's," Nick said.

Suddenly there was a loud commotion outside, the sound of men shouting and horses running.

"I think maybe we're about to find out," Clint said.

By the time Cactus Stone, Paul Nicholas, and Clint reached the undertaker's, the place looked like it was under siege. There were at least a dozen men on horseback in front, including Gary Lane and Travis Hollitt.

"What's goin' on?" Stone shouted.

"These men want to take Mr. Hollitt's body," the undertaker said.

"Go inside, George," Stone said, "I'll take care of it."

"You won't take care of anything, Cactus," Travis Hollitt said. "You're a joke as a lawman, so get out of the way. We're comin' in."

"I can't let you do that, Travis," Stone said. "Maybe I am a joke to you, but I'm still the law. I want all of you men to go home. Poor Mr. Hollitt is dead."

"I'll take that badge off of you myself, Cactus," Travis shouted.

"Go ahead, Travis," Stone said, "take it."

Hollitt stared at Stone for a few moments, and while he did Clint and Nick moved in to flank the sheriff and support him.

Finally, Travis Hollitt looked at Gary Lane and said, "Take his badge, Gary."

As Lane started to dismount, Clint shouted, "Why don't you take it yourself, Travis? Why have somebody do it for you?"

Hollitt glared at Clint. They both knew that Clint had backed him down once already, and now the man he called a joke of a sheriff was doing it, too.

"If Sheriff Stone is such a joke," Clint said, "why not come and take the badge yourself?"

"Yeah," Nick chimed in, "why send Lane to do your dirty work for you?"

"You want the badge, Gary?" Stone asked.

Gary Lane sat back in his saddle and regarded the three men critically.

"You men want to follow a man who can't do his own dirty work?" Stone asked.

"Or how about a man who keeps his sick father locked away in his room so he can take over the family business?" Clint asked.

"Or whose father is dead two days and he doesn't even know it?" Nick said.

"He told us you killed his father and stole the body," a man called out.

"If these men had killed Anson Hollitt," Stone said, "they'd be in my jail. You can all ask Doc who killed Anson. It was whoever kept him locked in his room and didn't get him any medical treatment."

"His own son and daughter," Clint said.

The men started to grumble and look at each other.

"Well, Travis?" Stone said. " Are you coming for my badge?"

Hollitt stared at Stone and said, "I thought we were friends, Cactus."

"The sad thing is," Stone said, "so did I, once."

FORTY-FIVE

As Amanda rode him up and down she was so wet they made sucking noises between them. Neither of them noticed, however, they were so caught up in each other. She had her head thrown back, and he moved his lips along her neck, down to the slopes of her breasts until he was sucking her nipples, first one, then the other. She gasped and came down on him and swiveled her hips. If they weren't in the barber chair she could have closed her thighs around him. Instead she dug her knees into his thighs and then almost leapt out of the chair as waves of pleasure pulsed through her. In the next second Clint groaned aloud and exploded inside of her, and they both almost fell out of the chair again. . . .

"Jesus," he said, dressing. "I didn't even have a chance to take a bath."

She smiled as she buttoned her dress.

"I wanted to get to you before you got to a bathtub," she said. "Now maybe one of the girls will have to work harder with you."

"I think I just might go for a regular bath."

He went in the back and told Joey just that, that he just wanted to soak.

"Amanda's given you a haircut already, is that it?" she asked.

"Well . . ."

She left him to his hot bath, and in the steaming water his thoughts drifted back . . .

He had just arrived in Dawson City that day, having left all of the tragedy behind him in Winter Creek. The whole town now knew that Anson Hollitt was dead. Word was getting out, and it was only a matter of time before they began to see what effect that had on business. However, the Hollitt mill might actually run into trouble even before that. Travis and Rachel weren't speaking when Clint left, because apparently Rachel blamed her brother for talking her into their plan. Travis was telling anyone who would listen that it was as much her fault as it was his. She was the one who was supposed to be taking care of the old man.

The foreman, Gary Lane, had quit and left town even before Clint did.

As for the letter which Anson never did get to read, just before leaving town Clint had gotten his answer to that from Martha, the cook in the Hollitt house.

"It's a shame what they did to that man," she said to Clint after Anson Hollitt's funeral. Clint had gone to the funeral, if only to represent Leonard Hollitt.

"Martha, do you know anything about Leonard Hollitt?"

"I do," she said. "I do, and I'm ashamed to say he was my grandson."

"What?"

Fresh tears ran down her face.

"My daughter came to work with me at the Hollitt house twenty years ago. She had gone off on her own and had no success, not with her acting career, and not with men. She came to the house, and immediately I knew there would be trouble."

"What kind of trouble?"

"Between Mr. Hollitt and Evelyn."

"There was trouble?"

"They started carrying on behind Mrs. Hollitt's back. I knew it and couldn't stop it."

"And Evelyn became pregnant?"

"Yes," Martha said. "Mr. Hollitt gave her money and made her leave. I probably should have left with her, but I was so angry at her."

"What about him? Weren't you angry at him?"

"I was, but I had worked for the family for so long. Where would I go?"

She could have gone with her daughter and helped her with her baby, Clint thought, but he didn't say that.

"When Leonard came back fifteen years later, calling himself Hollitt, I like to have died."

"And what happened?"

"The Hollitts used money again to take care of the problem. Leonard only wanted a father, but they pushed money on him and made him leave."

"They meaning Anson and his wife?"

"Oh no, Mrs. Hollitt had passed on by then. It was Mr. Hollitt and Travis. They didn't want no part of Leonard."

"And what about you, Martha?" he asked. "Did you want any part of Leonard?"

"God forgive me," she said, "no."

So the boy drifted for four years until he got to the point where he just wanted to die, and he picked Clint for the job. More than ever, now, Clint wished he had tried harder to talk Leonard out of it. Clint could have gone on with his life very happily without knowing what Anson Hollitt had done to Leonard, and then what Travis and Rachel Hollitt had done to Anson.

Very happily, indeed.

Clint finished his bath without another visit from Joey, feeling faintly disappointed that she hadn't come back and tried again. He thought that a talented girl like her probably would have had no trouble getting him back into a "haircut" mood.

He dressed and went back out into the barbershop, where Amanda was patiently waiting for her next customer.

"You look refreshed."

"I feel refreshed."

"Where are you heading from here?"

"I don't know," he said. "I'll just be heading. . . ."

"And your friend?"

"I don't know what he'll do after this, but he should be here in a few minutes for his bath."

"Does he know . . ."

"No, he thinks this is just a regular barbershop and bathhouse."

"This must be him now," she said, looking out the window. "My, he's a good-looking young man."

"Think we could make sure Joey takes care of him?"

"I think that can be arranged," she said, with a smile.

Paul Nicholas entered the barbershop and said to Clint, "Got your message that you'd be here. Hello, ma'am."

"Hello."

"You had your bath already?" Nick asked Clint.

"Yup. It's your turn."

"Maybe I should have a haircut and a shave first?"

"Uh, no," Clint said, "I think you should have your bath first. I'm going to get a shave now."

"Well, okay," Nick said. "I could really use a long, hot bath, Which way?"

"Right through that door," Clint said, pointing. "I don't think you'll be disappointed."

Watch for

THE LAST GREAT SCOUT

162nd novel in the exciting GUNSMITH series
from Jove

Coming in June!

J. R. ROBERTS

JUL ⎯ ⎯ 1995 # THE

GUNSMITH